Second Revolution

ANOTHER YEAR OF FLASH FICTION

Second Revolution

ANOTHER YEAR OF FLASH FICTION

Jamie Lackey

ISBN: 978-0-578-57406-6

Table of Contents

Females Aren't Welcome on Ether	9
The Ghost Girl and the Fox	13
A Flash of Scales	17
Beauty's Choice	21
Never Alone	25
Tomorrow	29
The New Normal	35
A Walk in the Park	41
The Princess and the Dragon	45
Alone Among the Trees	51
Unicorn Dreams	57
Charlie-Bird Saves Us All From the Alien Invaders, Or Bird Want Shiny	61
At the End of Everything, There is the Sea	65
Everyday Miracles	69
Gunpowder Plot	73
The Shape of Future Days	77
King of the Mushroom Forest	81
The Huntress	85
Vampires, Dirty Alleys, and Black Cats that Aren't	89
Restitution	93
Unravelling, a Guided Meditation	99
A Single Page Rescued from a Lady's Journal	103
A Christmas Legacy	105
A Midwinter Miracle	109

Bonus Stories

Down the River	113
Home Fires	115
A Leveraged Buyout	117
Progress	121
Afterword	127

This book is dedicated to everyone who backed my Indiegogo campaign. This book literally wouldn't exist without you.
Thank you!

Prompt #1

"Since you always destroy me over my misogynistic male leads, I want you to write a misogynistic male character who is likable. Maybe he's an old-timer having trouble adapting to the new ways of life, maybe he was deeply hurt by women in the past, I'll leave the details to you. Good luck (mwahahahaha)."

You might be able to guess from the prompt, but this one was a bit of a challenge. I started with it because I like to face adversity head on, I suppose.

Females Aren't Welcome on Ether

For Vince

Demetrius walked into his classroom and found the boys huddled together in whispered conversation.

"I heard that females were 20 feet tall, and that's why we don't have any—because they wouldn't fit in the spaceship."

"I heard that they all went crazy every full moon and would either throw things or start crying."

"I heard that they were just so physically weak that they couldn't move in Ether's gravity."

Demetrius cleared his throat, and the boys all scurried to their desks. "Are we ready for today's lesson?" he asked.

Wade spoke up without raising his hand. "Could you tell us why females aren't welcome on Ether?"

Demetrius was their history teacher, so he supposed that the question was at least somewhat on topic. "On Earth, there were all kinds of different people. Men, women, people who felt that they were both, or neither. People with dark skin, or light. And because of that, people were treated differently. Or so they claimed. Some people complained about discrimination, while some were accused of unearned privilege. All based on things they had no control over.

"So, Ether's founders decided that we would all be the same. With modern genetics and birthing pods, our society doesn't need women to bear children. And we certainly don't need people to be different colors. So, our founders eliminated those differences. On old Earth, we'd all be what they referred to as 'white men.'"

Colin, one of the quieter students, raised his hand. "What does 'unearned privilege' mean?"

"Some people claimed that other people benefited from the inequality that was rampant on Earth. Saying someone was privileged was a way to attack them, to accuse them of being one of those people."

Colin raised his hand again. "But what if they really were benefiting from the inequality? Was it still an attack if it was true?"

Demetrius nodded, doing his best to project confidence. "Yes, of course it was. Now, let's get to today's lesson."

*

After the school day was over, Demetrius went to the birthing center. His son was three months along, and Demetrius was counting the days till he could hold his little boy in his arms. He stood by the pod and talked in a quiet, soothing voice, telling the baby stories about his day.

"You know there's no research to confirm that there's any benefit from talking to the pod," a familiar and unwelcome voice said from behind him.

"What are you doing here?" Demetrius demanded. He'd won the lottery over Frank—the baby growing in the pod was his son, fair and square. There was no reason for Frank to visit.

"There's no rule saying I can't be here," Frank said.

"There's also no reason that you should be here," Demetrius snapped.

Frank shrugged. "Maybe I just wanted to see you."

They'd been close, once. But that was a long time ago. They'd drifted apart even before they'd had to compete for one of the coveted positions on the birthing center's new father list.

"Well, you've seen me. Now leave."

"Fine."

Frank stormed away. Demetrius spent a long time examining his pod, assuring himself that his son was healthy. The readings all looked normal. Still, Demetrius couldn't shake the feeling that something was wrong.

*

The months slipped by. Demetrius counted every day, till finally, finally, it was time to remove his son from the birthing pod.

The community was invited to every birth, so Demetrius wasn't surprised to see Frank there. He also wasn't pleased.

Still, there was nothing he could do but ignore Frank's unwelcome presence.

The birthing pod dinged, the amniotic goo drained away. Demetrius' son wriggled in his grasp as he pulled him out into the world. He kicked and waved his fists, then his eyes fastened on Demetrius's face, and he stared.

Demetrius's heart melted.

"There's something wrong with him," someone whispered.

Frank started to laugh.

Demetrius clutched his son to his chest. "What's going on?"

"It's a girl," Frank said.

10

Demetrius scanned his son's tiny body, and realized that Frank was right. His son—no, there was a different word for a girl-child. Doffter? Something close to that, surely. His baby was almost perfect, with ten fingers and ten toes, but there was something that was definitely missing.

"Females aren't welcome on Ether," Frank said. "It'll have to be eliminated."

"She," Demetrius said, remembering the female pronoun. "Not it. She." He blinked back tears, fought to keep his shaking knees steady.

One of the birthing techs stepped forward. "We're so sorry, we have no idea how this could have happened. Please, give us the mistake and we'll take care of it. You can have the next slot," he offered, holding out his arms.

"He can't have the next slot, that's not fair," Frank protested. "It should go to the lottery."

Demetrius could only assume that Frank had sabotaged the pod, somehow.

But it didn't matter. He looked down at his baby, and she looked back up at him.

Demetrius's doffter—no, his daughter, that was the word—gave a little hiccupping cry and curled her tiny fist into his shirt. He had no idea what human females were actually like, no idea if they did grow to be 20 feet tall, or if they lost their minds during the full moon, or if they were too weak to stand in Ether's gravity.

That last, at least, wouldn't be an issue.

"I won't give her to you. Or to anyone. We'll leave," he said.

"That is an acceptable solution," the tech said, stepping back.

"Don't be insane," Frank said. "You can't just take her and go, you have no idea what you're doing."

Frank was right—the thought of leaving, of being a father to a daughter instead of a son, of facing all of the unknowns beyond Ether's gravity well, it was all terrifying. But not as terrifying has handing her back.

Demetrius held his daughter close, and turned to face his future.

Prompt #2
"A story about chickens."

My mother grew up on a chicken farm and one of my best friends has chickens now, so I have just enough second-hand chicken knowledge to be going on with.

The Ghost Girl and the Fox

For Debbie

Amber drifted a few feet away from the chicken coop as her younger sister knelt to gather a pair of grayish blue eggs. "There are a few more over behind that bit of hay," she said, even though she knew that her sister couldn't hear her.

When the eggs were gathered, she followed her sister as far from the chicken coop as she could. She made it about a quarter of the way to the house, then whatever tethered her to the chicken coop pulled her up short. She sighed. At least her range didn't seem to be shrinking.

The chickens couldn't see her any more than her living family members could, but the foxes responded when she charged at them. She'd named the oblivious chickens and did her best to protect them.

She couldn't protect her family, but she could at least keep their egg supply safe.

Roland was still renting the spare bedroom over her father's study. She sometimes saw him striding about, his smile as sharp as any fox's.

It was possible that he'd stop after killing just her, that he wasn't a habitual murderer.

But Amber doubted it. He'd seemed so horrifyingly competent at it with his hand locked around her throat.

She didn't even know why he'd killed her. That, she felt, was a bad sign as well.

A fox approached from the woods, but he stopped outside of her limited range. He sat and regarded her with a vulpine grin.

"Hello there, ghost girl," he said.

If Amber had still been alive, she would have been shocked to be addressed by a fox. But being dead seemed to have deadened her emotions, like they had a wet woolen blanket draped over them. "Good morning."

"It'd be a better morning if you'd like me have one of those chickens."

Henrietta and Bloopy wandered past Amber's legs, pecking at the hard ground. They didn't even notice the fox. "No, sorry."

"How about an egg?"

"Nope."

"How about an egg in trade for a favor?"

"What favor?" Amber asked.

The fox gave a little shrug. "What do you want?"

Amber hadn't really wanted much since she died. But she worried about her sisters. "If you can find out why Roland killed me, I'll let you have an egg."

"That's a bit of a challenge," the fox said.

"Do you not think you can do it?" Amber asked. She supposed it would be a difficult task for a fox.

The fox bristled. "I can do anything."

Amber smiled. "Oh, good."

"I'll go find out right now," the fox said. "Make sure you find me an egg."

*

Amber had forgotten about the fox when he came back a few days later. He was missing a patch of fur on his bushy tail. "He's a mean one, your Roland," he said.

"I'd hardly call him mine," Amber said. "I wasn't fond of him even before he murdered me."

"As to that, I think he's just a bit of a madman. He killed you because he could."

Amber nodded, remembering the look in his eyes. "Well, I suppose you've earned your egg." She pointed at one that was tucked under the chicken coop.

The fox scarfed the egg down in two bites. "How many eggs could I have if I get him to come down here so that you can deal with him?"

"Ten," Amber said, though she wasn't sure what she'd be able to do to Roland. Frightening foxes was one thing, a man who couldn't even see her was something else again.

"Ten, eh? Sounds fair," the fox said, just as heavy footfalls pounded down the path from the house.

Roland dove for the fox, his face twisted into a familiar angry snarl.

The fox evaded him easily.

Amber regarded Roland, on his belly in the dust. "It might take some time to gather all ten."

"Understood," the fox said.

Amber sank a hand into Roland's shoulder. She'd never tried touching the chickens, or her sisters. But there had to be some reason why the foxes feared her.

Touching Roland was like putting her hand into a sink full of hot water, just shy of scalding.

Roland gasped in pain. He tried to scramble away, but he couldn't see her, so it was easy for her to stay close. He kept pushing his whole body through her, which was unpleasant for her. It seemed to be much worse for him. He didn't even get close to the limit of her range.

His skin was starting to look a little gray, and the feel of him was more lukewarm than hot.

Eventually, he stopped moving. Amber hovered, waiting to see if his ghost emerged. But there was nothing.

Amber felt a wave of joy. She'd done it! She'd protected her family. She felt herself starting to let go, to move on. A comforting force tugged her toward whatever it was that came next.

The chickens squawked behind her. She turned and saw Bloopy hanging from the fox's bloody jaws. He nodded to her.

Amber wondered if this had all been to his plan all along. But it wasn't her problem anymore. And anyway, she'd promised ten eggs that she wouldn't be able to deliver.

She nodded back to the fox, and faded away.

Prompt #3
"Sea dragons, real or magical."

To literally no one's surprise, I decided to go with magical sea dragons.

A Flash of Scales

For Amy

When I was born, I wriggled free from my translucent egg just like the rest of my sisters. But as they swam effortlessly away, twisting and spinning through the water in an effortless dance, I floundered. Because where they had beautiful tails covered with bioluminescent scales, I had legs.

Our mother, exhausted after protecting her eggs, slipped into the depths. My sisters scattered, seeking prey, hungry from the struggle of hatching.

I attempted to follow, but quickly found myself alone. I swam up, through water that grew brighter and brighter around me. I lunged for any fish I saw, but they dodged away, leaving behind nothing but a flash of scales.

I would have starved quickly if not for the sea dragon. "I did not think I'd see the like of you again," she said, her voice so deep that I could hear it with my bones. She twined her way toward me, flowing through the water like she was a current given flesh.

"The likes of me?" I asked. The sound of my own voice surprised me. I'd never had an occasion to speak before.

"Your kind are born as a bridge between the peoples of the land and sea. You're able to live in both places, but you're not well adapted to either." She moved almost faster than I could see, snatching a fish between her glistening teeth. She dropped into my hands. "What is your name?"

My mother had whispered names to each of her daughters, while she fought off any threat to our vulnerable eggs and slowly starved. "Naupaka."

"I am Montsechia. Come, I will teach you how to survive."

*

She told me how to fashion a spear, how to wait, floating perfectly still, till my prey was in easy striking distance. She taught me how to smash open crab's shells, and how to tell what plants were safe to eat. She showed me places where fish gathered to spawn, introduced me to pods

17

of friendly dolphins who would let me cling to their fins while they swam so much faster than I could, no matter how hard I kicked.

I never once thought to wonder why. She taught, and I learned. That was just how things worked.

*

I was gathering kelp near the surface—higher than other mermaids usually ventured—when one of my sisters approached me. "Are you Naupaka? The sea dragon's pet?"

"Montsechia is my teacher," I said. "I'm her student, not her pet."

"You aren't a tribe. Not equals. Student or pet, it hardly matters."

"What do you want?"

"My tribe needs the sea dragon's help. There is a poison in the water."

"Why come to me? Why not just ask her?"

"Why take the risk of her refusing, when I can take you and demand her help?"

My sister lunged for me. She was still faster, but I pushed her away with my spear. I swam away, up and up, to where the water was so bright it hurt even my eyes.

She fell away behind me, but I kept going, up and up, till I ran out of water and broke into the air.

My lungs inflated automatically, but my ribs ached at the unfamiliar expansion, and the unfiltered light stung my eyes and skin.

I looked around at the unbroken horizon, at the unwavering blue of the sky. I laughed, and my voice was alien and strange in my ears. Then a hand wrapped around my ankle and pulled me back down.

*

Montsechia came for me, as I knew she would. "Are you unhurt?" she asked.

I nodded. My sister was worse off than I was—the light had left her fair skin red and tender. "We'll give you your pet back once the poison is gone," she said.

Montsechia ignored her, and kept her eyes on mine. "I can fix their problem, or I can kill them. Which would you prefer?"

"The poison might spread. I think it would be best to help."

"You are kind, Naupaka." Montsechia's eyes flicked to my sister for the first time. "And you are lucky."

As we swam away together, afterwards, I turned to her—my teacher, my friend, my surrogate mother, my savior—and asked, "Why did you decide to help me?"

18

She didn't pretend to not understand, didn't ask what I meant. "I planned to ask you go to go the surface for me, when you were strong enough. I am curious what has become of the humans."

"I thought they were gone." I thought I was a bridge with only one end, that cantilevered into nothingness.

"They were poisoning the ocean, so I drove them from it. I expect at least some of them still live, somewhere far from the shore. Maybe they have learned wisdom. Maybe they have not. Maybe your birth is a sign. Maybe it is not."

"Why didn't you ask me to go?" I asked. "I'm strong enough now."

"I suppose you are," she said. "It has been good, being your teacher. Not being alone. You don't have to go, if you don't want to. No matter what, I'll never regret giving you that first fish. You have been a joy to me, Naupaka."

"I have never stood on my feet," I said. "I think I'd like to."

"Very well," she said, and she led me to the shore.

I floundered as I pushed myself free from the surf. But after a few steps I began to understand how to balance my weight, how to press one foot into the sand and lift the other.

I turned, and waved, and watched Montsechia slip into the depth, leaving behind nothing but a flash of scales.

Then I filled my lungs with air and walked inland.

Prompt #4
"A Beauty and the Beast retelling."

I love fairy tale retellings. Something about a familiar story told in a new way appeals to me.

Beauty's Choice

For Paul

Tiny magical lights gleamed between glossy summer leaves, and the scent of roses hung heavy in the night air. It was a lovely night for a romantic stroll. Or for an escape attempt. Beauty had left her silk gown and satin shoes behind in favor of stolen trousers and her own well-worn boots. She darted over the moss-covered garden paths, past the bubbling fountain and crumbling statues, to the one tree that grew close to the exterior wall.

She'd delayed her escape attempt again and again out of fear of this climb. She'd spent dozens of secret, sweaty hours on the sumptuous carpet of her luxurious room, exercising to build up strength in her arms.

She'd never climbed a tree. She'd been a scholarly girl, not one to run off and roughhouse with the village boys.

Her delay had nearly cost her her will. The palace—it was not her home, though it was frighteningly tempting to call it that—was lovely, the invisible servants with their soft hands and soft whispers were kind in their heartbreaking way. But Beauty would not be their caged bird.

She jumped and reached for the lowest limb. Bark scraped her palms, but she couldn't grip the branch. She fell and hit the ground hard. Pain spiked through her hip and her breath left her body in a rush.

She tried again and ripped two fingernails on her left hand. But on the third try, her grip held. She strained up, kicking her legs. Her arms trembled, but she managed to pull herself up into the tree.

She clung to the trunk and stood slowly, her knees shaking.

The next part was easier, leveraging herself up one branch at a time, grateful for the weight she'd lost during the first weeks when she refused to eat.

She glanced over and could see past the wall. But instead of familiar forest paths or even tangled woods, the world dropped away to a rocky cliff with moonlit waves lapping the rocks far below. Her courage nearly failed her.

But even though she'd never climbed a tree before, she was a strong swimmer. She took a deep breath, then jumped from the tree to the top of the wall.

In the moment that she hung in the air, suspended between wood and stone, heavy footsteps pounded down the garden path.

"Beauty!" the Beast's voice was anguish.

She teetered on the wall, arms wind-milling.

"Please," he called, "I need you."

He was not the monster that he seemed—Beauty knew that now—and the pain in his voice tore at her heart.

She sat down on top of the wall and pulled off her boots. She dropped one and watched it fall and fall. It vanished into the shadows before splashing into the waves below.

"So you could never love me, then?" the Beast asked, his voice dulled by heartbreak.

Beauty stood. "I could. I might already."

"I don't understand."

"I've lost track of how long I've been here, with only you to care about. It is hard to remember anyone else's face. You stole my life, and gave me yourself in return. I can feel myself becoming the person you want me to be."

"You don't have to become anything for me. I don't care who you are, as long as you stay. I love you, Beauty. This stopped being about the curse for me a long time ago."

"It would be easy to love you, easy to stay here in this palace." A part of her wanted that so, so badly. And that, more than anything else, filled the rest of her with rage and fear. "But I still make my own choices. And I choose to go."

"And what if I choose to follow you?" he asked.

"That's up to you," Beauty said. She looked down, one last time, into his eyes. They were kind and sad in his monstrous face. She dove. The wind whistled past her ears, then she hit the water and swam.

Prompt #5
"Glimpse of a few select disparate days of an immortal consciousness that takes over bodies of people that were about to die anyway and attempts positive change for the people in that person's life."

This was such an interesting prompt, and it was a lot of fun to come up with an idea for.

Never Alone

For Nick

The ghost believed that she'd once had memories of her own—that she'd seen the world through her own eyes, felt the breeze with her own skin. That she'd had her own hopes and dreams and passions.

She believed that her sense of self might have even lasted through her first few inhabitations. But now, as her essence settled into Patricia Willis and Patricia's entire memory surged through her like a flood, there was nothing left of the ghost's original self to wash away.

The ghost had a feeling, not quite a memory, but a solid feeling, that she'd once tried to count the people she helped. But the number had grown beyond counting and slipped from her mind.

The ghost drew a breath into Patricia's lungs, settled into Patricia's pain. She was on her back in a hospital bed, as she so often was, attached to various machines that beeped and hummed. Fluorescent lights painted the world around her in flat shades of white and beige.

A young woman dozed beside the bed, and the ghost felt a wave of Patricia's conflicted anguish. She lifted Patricia's hand and touched her daughter's smooth cheek.

And then she said the words that Patricia would have never been able to say. "I'm so sorry, Lisa."

Lisa's eyes filled with tears, and she gave a choked sob as she took Patricia's hand between her own.

"You're a wonderful daughter, and I'm sorry that I refused to see it."

"It's okay. I love you, Mom."

The ghost curled Patricia's fingers around Lisa's and squeezed once. Then she let go.

*

The ghost wasn't sure how much time passed between her inhabitations. If one followed an instant after the next, or if she floated, thoughtless and formless, for moments uncounted until she was called.

She settled into Thomas Butler, who was standing in the middle of a sunlit street. A pickup truck squealed around the corner, and the ghost

25

used Thomas's arms to push his little brother away, watched as the smaller boy stumbled up onto the sidewalk, into safety. Then pain.

Then nothing.

*

She wondered what happened to the souls that she helped, afterwards. Did they pass beyond some barrier into some kind of afterlife? Did they fade away into nothing? Did they join her, jumping from one death to the next to the next?

The ghost settled into Andrea Lee. Cold water pummeled her from every direction, stinging her eyes, choking her. The only light came from a sliver of moon, peaking through scuttling clouds.

Sometimes, there were no bridges to repair, no lives to save. Andrea's body was exhausted, and the ghost could do nothing to stop the tide's tireless pull.

But Andrea wasn't alone, and the ghost hoped that mattered.

She turned Andrea's face toward the moon and watched the lacy pattern of the clouds. She floated for as long as she could, then she sank into darkness.

*

The ghost joined Skylar Jackson on a battlefield in the desert, and she did what she always did when she found herself holding a gun.

She lowered it.

*

She didn't know if she was doing the right things. She had a sense that she'd had a mission, once. But it was gone with her name and her memories. She wondered if she'd ever be able to rest, or if she'd just keep dying over and over and over.

But at least she was never alone. And to the ghost, that mattered.

26

Prompt #6
"Time Loops"

I adore time loop stories. But I'm not sure if I've ever read a flash fiction story that managed time loops before, so this was a bit of a challenge. I feel like I got away with it, though.

Tomorrow

For Patrick

Amber opened her eyes. Sunlight and cold air streamed in through the broken window, and Tenesha was crying in the next room over.

She'd stop in a minute.

Amber got up. She brushed her teeth. There was no point to it, but she enjoyed feeling fresh and minty for a few moments.

This time, she tried sneaking into the embassy and talking to the alien's ambassador. She'd already tried everyone in her own government. Over and over and over again.

It didn't work.

But at least the aliens didn't torture her before they killed her.

*

Amber opened her eyes. She was cold. Tenesha was crying.

She was running out of ideas.

If she waited long enough, Tenesha would come in with breakfast. Two pieces of toast with cake frosting, since they were out of peanut butter. Tenesha would take her hand and tell her that everything would be okay, even though her eyes were red and her breath smelled like whisky.

Amber got up, got dressed, walked out.

She spent the day observing. Memorizing. There was a boy buying flowers for his mother who always made her smile. He'd glance between one bouquet of roses and another, like the choice mattered, like his mother love either one less than the other.

She went home before the blast. Tenesha stood with her hands on her hips in the living room. "Where have you been, young lady?"

Amber just hugged her. Explaining never did any good. Fighting never did any good. "We can talk about it tomorrow," she said.

She wondered when her mother had started to seem so young.

*

Amber opened her eyes. At least it was a lovely, sunny day after the cold morning. It could be worse.

She'd heard once that Bill Murry's character in *Groundhog Day* had lived the equivalent of thousands of years repeating the same day over and over and over. In all that time, he'd never seen the sun.

It was really no wonder he went crazy for a bit.

Amber had no idea how long it had been. But she'd taught herself how to hack into the alien's systems, how to break into government offices, how to speak four languages. How to get people to trust you when you were telling them truths they didn't want to hear. How to get them to trust you when you lied.

But she only had a day to fix peace talks that had been falling apart for years. Decades, maybe.

She was starting to worry that one day wasn't enough, no matter how many times you repeat it.

*

Amber opened her eyes.

She went back to the alien embassy over and over, till she had a path to the ambassador's office. "Please," she said. "Please stop them from destroying my planet."

The ambassador glared at her, its black eyes glistening. Its gray-green skin looked dry and flaky, probably from the stress. "How did you get in here?"

"That doesn't matter. What matters is the bomb your people are preparing to drop on this planet."

"What are you talking about?"

Amber sighed. "Look, I know that you don't want this. Is there anything anyone can do to change their minds?"

The ambassador sagged. "I don't know. I don't have time to figure it out."

"I have time. Mindlink with me, I'll try to figure it out."

Amber didn't want to mindlink with one of the aliens about to destroy her planet. Mindlinks were invasive and horrible and changed you forever.

But she had tried on her own for so long, and had gotten nowhere.
She was tired.

"I'm sorry, child, I don't know what you think you know or how you know it, but you do not have time."

"What would I have to say to you to get you to mindlink with me?"

"You'd have to be the love of my life," the alien snapped. "Now get out before I call security.

*

Amber opened her eyes. She gave herself the morning. Let Tenesha bring her toast with frosting and walked for a bit in the sunshine.

Then she went back to the ambassador's office.

"Hi. I'm the love of your life," she said. "You have to mindlink with me so that we can save this planet together."

The ambassador closed its eyes. Opened them again. "Fuck it," it said, and took her face in its hands.

*

Amber opened her eyes. The room was still cold, Tenesha was still crying. But she was different.

She went back to the ambassador. Thav'rek'li. Amber knew its name now. Its name, its story, its dreams.

It didn't know her.

She'd been afraid that knowing everything else about another living being would feel overwhelming, but she'd lived such a very long time that there was no danger of its memories overloading her own.

But it had been nice, for a few hours. Having an equal. Someone who just knew everything she'd been through. Someone who understood.

Amber hadn't cried in a long, long time, and she wouldn't now.

*

Amber opened her eyes, then closed them again. She'd use what Thav'rek'li had given her, and she'd come up with a plan. Not matter how long it took.

*

Amber opened her eyes and listened to Tenesha cry. She wondered what she'd give to wake up to something else.

*

Amber opened her eyes and wondered what she'd give to just not wake up again at all.

Amber opened her eyes. She had a plan. And eventually, it would work.

"Hi Thav'rek'li," she said as she slipped into its office. "We need to kidnap your queen. If she's here, they can't blow up the planet."

"Who are you? How you know my name?"

"I'll explain everything tomorrow. Are you going to help me or not?"

*

Amber opened her eyes, got up, and tried again.

*

Amber opened her eyes and screamed at the sunshine and the broken window and Tenesha's sobs. Then she tried again.

*

Amber opened her eyes. The room was dark and warm and quiet, and she was chained to a wall. She could just barely see Thav'rek'li, chained to the wall across from her. "It's tomorrow," the ambassador said.

Amber told the love of her life everything, and cried.

Prompt #7
"Helping a friend through a hard time, maybe with superhero?"

Absolutely with a superhero. I love superhero stories, they are always such fun.

The New Normal

To my friend Chris, I will always be here to help. -Branden

Joseph ran up his front steps two at a time. "Meena? I'm home, where are you?" She wasn't in the kitchen, or her office, or the bedroom. "Honey? I got your text, what's going on?"

He found her phone, plugged in next to the bed, still showing her message—*I need you, come home now*—and all of his unread, increasingly frantic replies.

He found her in the garden, surrounded by what looked like all of the deer that roamed their suburban neighborhood and a few stray cats.

"They're mine now. I can see through all of their eyes, make them do what I want," she said as he rushed out of the house. "I want to see if you can be mine, too."

She took his hand, and everything around him wobbled.

Her laugh sounded like it came from everywhere. "I can! This is amazing! What else can I do?"

A tiny, unimportant corner of his mind realized that she had superpowers, now, and that the sudden strain had cracked her, like it had so many others since the Emergence.

He stood by while she pulled more and more creatures under her thrall, till she attracted the notice of the local team of super heroes.

Then she used him, just like everything else that she controlled, when the heroes fought her.

Then she was in a crumpled heap on the ground, and everything went black.

*

Joseph went through all the right motions at the funeral. He shook hands, hugged people, nodded when they offered condolences. He might even have shed a tear or two at the appropriate moments, he wasn't sure. When it was all over, he couldn't really remember much of it.

The doctors said that his mind would return to normal, eventually. That his life would stop feeling like something he was watching without much interest instead of something that he was living.

That eventually, he wouldn't be Meena's anymore.

"Do you want me to take you home?" Stewart, his best friend, asked when everyone else had gone.

Joseph shrugged. He knew he should care, or at least pretend to, but he was tired. He's been pretending to care all day.

"Meena really did a number on you, huh," Stewart said, taking Joseph's arm and clearly not expecting an answer as he guided him to the car. "Super scary, what supers can do when they crack."

Joseph grunted in agreement. It was scary, he supposed. It hadn't felt scary at the time though. He'd been a part of something larger than himself, and he'd felt... complete.

Stewart took him home and made him some scrambled eggs. "Look, man, I know things are hard for you right now, but I'm here. You know that, right? I can stay with you for as long as you need me."

Joseph nodded. He did know.

"Do you want to talk or anything?"

"Not yet." Maybe not ever. He wasn't sure.

"How about we watch a movie, then? Something to get you out of your own head for a bit."

"Yeah. That sounds good."

*

The deer and cats and other creatures that Meena had pulled in were still hanging around the yard. If Joseph hadn't fully thrown off her hold yet, how could the animals hope to do it?

He liked having them there. It made him feel a little more whole.

Then one morning, Stewart found him sleeping on the ground outside, curled between two deer with a vole or something tucked under his chin. Joseph didn't remember going outside. But he already knew that his memory wasn't the best.

"This is worrying." Stewart said, making more eggs. "I mean, even aside from the weird brain stuff. What about fleas? Or ticks? You do not want Lyme disease on top of everything else."

One of the pack was a possum, he remembered. Possums ate ticks, right? He should be able to have it check on the others.

Joseph opened his mouth to tell Stewart that, then stopped. "I think you should take me to get tested," he said instead.

"Tested for Lyme?"

"No, for super powers."

Stewart quietly let the nurse make some very wrong assumptions about their relationship so that he could stay in the room while Joseph waited for the doctor. "I'd understand if you didn't want to stay," he said.

"Not everyone cracks," Stewart said. "I trust you."

"I trusted Meena."

Stewart shrugged. "What she did was messed up, but I don't think she meant to hurt you."

"Yeah, so even if I didn't mean to hurt you, things could still get pretty bad."

"I'm not going anywhere. I said I was here for you, and I meant it." They sat in silence for a moment. Then Stewart added, "This is probably better than talking about feelings, anyway."

Joseph laughed. "You're so full of shit."

The test was straightforward, but the results were inconclusive. "Well, something weird is going on," the doctor said. "It's unclear if you're manifesting a separate power of your own, or if this development is a lingering result of your wife's influence."

"I'm not getting any better."

"We can schedule regular appointments to monitor the situation, but at the moment, I don't feel like any further action is necessary."

*

Joseph sat out on the porch, surrounded by his animals. He wondered when he'd stopped thinking of them as Meena's.

Stewart brought him a beer. "You're wrong about one thing, you know," he said.

"What's that?"

"You are getting better. Like, the weird animal thing isn't going away, but you're—you're better than you were. Not so far away anymore. You actually laughed today. I can't remember the last time that happened. Maybe the menagerie is doing you some good."

"Having a psychic connection with a bunch of deer has to be the stupidest superpower ever."

"Now, now. It's not just deer. There are also some rodents and a few cats."

"You're right. That definitely makes it better."

They sat on the porch, surrounded by Joseph's menagerie of suburban wildlife, and watched the sun go down. "Here's to the new normal," Stewart toasted.

Joseph nodded once, and clinked his bottle against Stewart's. Things weren't good, yet. But they certainly could be worse. "To the new normal."

Prompt #8
"Knee surgery recovery."

This was another somewhat difficult prompt. I struggled a bit with how to get an engaging story out of it, but it was an interesting challenge.

A Walk in the Park

For Chris

"We're terribly sorry again about all this."

Francis nodded to indicate that he'd heard, and continued to attempt to breathe through the pain. It seemed like a nonsense instruction, and didn't seem to be helping, but his body did require oxygen to function, so he kept at it.

"Your body is absolutely still under warranty."

Francis would hope so—he hadn't even been incorporated for an hour before his knee had twisted beneath him and he'd fallen in a heap.

"We'd like to offer two options. The first is a full body replacement. It will, unfortunately, take some time to grow a new body for you, but we would be happy to host your consciousness on our servers at no cost during that wait. The other option is to repair the damage to your current body. That would also be at no cost to you, of course. The recovery time after the surgery would not count toward the completion of your current contract, and we'd extend that contract for a full two years at no extra cost as an apology."

Francis had waited a long time for this body. He'd been so excited to get started living his incorporated life, and the thought of only spending a few hours in his body before being uploaded again was distressing. But the pain was really quite terrible. Of course he'd heard stories about pain, but he'd never imagined it could be so bad. "Will the surgery and recovery be painful? Is rehab difficult?"

"You would be placed under anesthetic for the surgery itself and be provided with pain medicine to help you through the recovery period. And rehab is a walk in the park!" The rep laughed. "Not literally. But it's designed to be as easy as possible!"

"Wait, there's medicine that helps with pain? Why wasn't I given any of that?"

"We wanted your mind to be clear when you made your choice."

"And you don't think excruciating pain is a mental impairment?" Francis certainly did. He couldn't make an important decision like this. He couldn't weigh the pros and cons—it was all he could do to keep breathing. In and out and in again. Sometimes he forgot which step he was on, and tried to inhale or exhale twice in a row, which did not work well at all.

"If you do keep your current body, you should be able to use the recovery time to get used to being incorporated. And two extra years is quite a value."

Francis shifted his weight, and the wheels of his wheelchair creaked ominously.

"You will also have a unique experience to share when your contract is up and you are re-uploaded."

That was a valid point. It would be nice to have a unique experience to add to his resume. "Is two years the best you can do? I am in quite a lot of pain, you understand."

The rep nodded sympathetically. "I stubbed my toe once. It was truly unpleasant. Let me reach out to my supervisor and see what I can do for you."

Francis contemplated the gulf of scope between a subbed toe and a whole series of torn ligaments while the rep conferred with her supervisor. He suspected that it was a vast difference, and he found himself preening a little, even through the pain. It would be something to be special.

"We can do three years, and we can throw in a sports upgrade to your body that we can install during your surgery. Here is our list of sports, if you'd like to pick one."

Francis went with swimming—something low-impact felt wise—and agreed to the terms.

*

Francis woke up after the surgery feeling sore all over from the sports upgrade in addition to the burning ache in his knee.

A bright pink nursebot rolled up to the bed. "Good morning, how are you feeling? Could you rate your pain on a scale of 1 to 10?"

Francis compared his pain to the agony that had immediately followed the injury. "5, I suppose."

"That is a great number!" the nursebot chirped. "I am sure you will be up and about in no time! Would you allow me to transfer you to your rehab station?"

"Yeah, I guess that's fine."

The nursebot scooped him up and carried him to a large, open room with large black machines. It placed him gently inside one, then closed it around him, so that only his head protruded. "Feel free to make a fist to pause the program if it is ever too intense."

All of the other machines were empty, except one in the far corner, which contained a woman whose face was twisted with pain.

She opened her eyes and tried to smile. "Hey there. I'm Carol. What are you in for?"

"My knee was improperly crafted," he said, then gasped as the machine started manipulating his joint. "How about you?"

"Broke my leg skydiving. Would have been an instant re-upload if I'd been reckless, but it was the company's fault. Equipment failure. So they gave me the option of fixing it. I like this body. It's my third, and my favorite so far, so I decided to keep it."

The conversation was a good distraction from the pain, he found. It was good to have something else to focus on. "This is my first time in a body."

"Oh, extreme pain right of the bat, huh? That is rough."

"I'm hoping it'll give me some distinction. Make me a little special."

"I suppose it will sound good, but no one else will really understand. I had an accident in my second body, only experienced the pain for a few second before I was re-uploaded. And whenever I mentioned it, people compared it to times they scraped their knee or banged an elbow on the shower door."

"It will look good on my resume, at least. And I am getting three extra years." Francis tried to believe that was worth it, while the rehab machine pulled and pressed and twisted. The pain spiked to a 9, and he cried out and closed his fist.

"It'll be worth it," Carol said. "The memory of the pain will fade. It always does."

"I hope you're right."

"What were you looking forward to about having a body?" Carol asked. "What are you going to do first when you get out of here?"

The pain ebbed back to a 5, and Francis let the machine continue. "I'm going to go for a walk in the park."

Prompt #9
"Spring and flowers."

This story is set in the same world as my novella, *The Forest God*. The novella itself was inspired by the spring, so it just felt right. It's such a wonderful world, and I really enjoy adding to it.

The Princess and the Dragon

For Linda, from Vicky

The Witch walked through the woods. Old snow lay in crusty patches of shade, and the wind that came down from the mountain was cold, but dainty snowdrops clustered together, bashfully turning their flowery faces toward the ground.

She wandered from one patch of flowers to the next, harvesting a handful of blossoms from each, till the basket that she carried overflowed, and the air around her filled with their soft, sweet scent.

She walked for a bit longer, her feet finding familiar paths, enjoying the spring sunshine on her face. Then she caught a flash of red among the gray and brown and creeping green of the spring wood.

She pushed off of the path, her feet crunching and sliding in the thick layer of fallen leaves.

The heady scent of roses overrode the snowdrops in her arms and the loam and leaves under her feet, and she found herself before an ancient twisted tree, its furrowed, coal-black bark almost completely covered with thick thorny vines and hundreds of bright red roses, each bigger than the palm of her hand.

The Witch had never seen such roses before, but the previous Witch had told stories of wicked flowers that bloomed when the Dragon woke.

As the Witch watched, the rosebush spread, vines slowly snaking across the ground, with new blossoms erupting from bud to flower in minutes instead of days.

She dropped her basket and picked one of the flowers, careful to avoid the jagged thorns. The petals crumbled to ash that scattered in the cold spring wind.

"Well," the Witch muttered, turning the blackened stem in her hands, "that isn't good."

*

Princess Marilla stood with her three older sisters before their father and mother, who looked incredibly grim. They had banished everyone but one poorly-dressed stranger from the throne room, so it was just the seven of them in the cavernous gold-and-marble room.

"There is news," the King said.

"Grave news," the Queen added.

"The Witch has told us that the Dragon has returned. As we have no sons to battle it, we must sacrifice one of our daughters."

Everyone knew that the King and Queen wished each of their daughters had been sons instead, but Marilla felt they blamed her the most for her femininity. She had been their last chance, after all.

"I suppose I should get changed. What does one wear to be sacrificed to a dragon?"

Her sisters turned to her, their eyes bright with tears. "Oh Marilla, how noble of you to volunteer!" her oldest sister cried.

Her parents' eyes were cold and dry, and Marilla knew that she had always been the one destined to go, whether she volunteered or not.

Her sisters hugged her and cried, but none of them offered to go in her place.

The Witch regarded her with her kind, understanding eyes. "I will guide you to the Dragon's cave," she said.

"Thank you," Marilla said. "I would hate to have to go alone."

*

The Princess donned a long white dress and a silver crown, and the Witch walked beside her through the city. People followed them, whispering, but no one spoke to the Princess. There were no cheers, no grateful shouts. They walked away from the city walls, over the arching bridge that crossed the river. The Witch glanced back to see that the crowd had dispersed. Not a single person had waited for then to vanish out of sight.

"It was very brave of you to volunteer," the Witch said.

The Princess shrugged. "One does what one must."

They reached the rose tree, and the Princess's steps faltered. She stared, entranced. "What beautiful flowers."

The Witch supposed they were beautiful, but she could only see the wrongness in them.

The Princess reached out and picked one.

It stayed fresh and lovely in her hand, and she smiled at it.

"They are Dragon Roses," the Witch said, expecting the Princess to drop the flower.

Instead, she lifted her chin. "Then I suppose I am free to take as many as I wish."

The Princess harvested roses, and none of the thorns pieced her soft skin. She gathered a bouquet so large that she had to hold the flowers between both hands.

"It's kind of the Dragon to give me roses before it eats me," she said, inhaling their fragrance. "I've always loved roses. They're my favorite flower."

"You seem very calm about getting eaten."

"It's the cycle, isn't it? I thought the Witch was all about the cycle. You sacrificed your name to become the Witch, didn't you?"

"My name is not quite the same as my life."

The Princess shrugged again. "I was never allowed the luxury of considering my life my own."

The Witch did not like the thought of sacrificing this girl. "There must be another way," she said.

"I cannot fight the Dragon. Even if I were a Prince instead of a Princess, I don't think I'd want that."

"Why not?"

"I think it must be lonely, being the only one of its kind," the Princess said. "If that has made it cruel, that's only fair."

They reached the edge of the woods and walked on, up the rocky path, leaving the trees behind them.

*

Marilla gripped her roses tight to keep her hands from trembling. Her heart raced in her chest as she took one step, then another.

The Witch was an unexpected comfort. She hadn't expected anyone to care about her.

Curls of smoke drifted across the path, and Marilla breathed in the scent of her roses.

The Dragon waited outside the mouth of its cave. Its scales were the same blood red as the roses, and its eyes the deep green of their vines. She thought she did see loneliness there, in its eyes.

It wasn't as huge as she'd imagined—its body was only twice as big as a large horse, and its scaly, horned head would fit in her lap if she knelt before it.

It was not nearly big enough to swallow her in one bite.

"So, they had no Prince to fight me," the Dragon said. "They have always sent a Prince before."

"We have no princes," Marilla said. "Just me. Thank you for the roses."

The Dragon blinked at her for a moment, then rumbled, "You are welcome."

Marilla stepped forward till she could feel the heat of its body radiating like a banked fire. "I offer myself up, as is required. But please, I should not like to suffer any more than is necessary." She was shaking now, and her hands unsteady. Every instinct screamed at her to flee.

But she would not.

The Dragon regarded her for a long moment, its green eyes bright. It held out a clawed hand. "You will not suffer," it said. "You have my word."

Marilla thrust her roses into the Witch's hands, and reached out her own toward the dragon.

As she touched it, her own hands changed. In an instant, her hands matched the Dragon's, their clawed and scaled fingers twined together.

"Come," the Dragon said, its eyes no longer lonely, and launched itself into the air.

Marilla followed, and they were flying.

*

The Witch held the Princess's bouquet. The stems were smooth in her hands, and the blooms remained fresh and beautiful.

She watched the dragons soar together, then went back to her woods.

The rosebush was gone, vanished as if it had never existed. The Witch picked up her basket, replaced her wilted snowdrops with the Princess's roses, and went back to her duties.

Overhead, two dragons soared together, and everything was in balance again.

Prompt #10
"Something in the ballpark of Stephen King-style horror* with a female lead."

This prompt also included a brilliant list of common Stephen King elements, which I was incredibly grateful for, since I've only read a handful of his works.

Alone Among the Trees

For my awesome mom, Zina Scott, from Jenn

For a little while after The Event, the state parks were more crowded. Kory remembered counting the people she met on the hiking trail, resentful of each one, till she got to an even dozen and gave up bothering. But as the weeks and years dragged by, everyone settled back into their accustomed complacency, and she could again count on her solitude when she retreated to the woods.

She was out re-blazing hiking trails and scraping away any gypsy moth eggs that she found when Gerri Wallace stepped out of a beech tree, her long hair wet and dripping, her older brother's flannel shirt hanging off of her in tattered rags. She looked real and solid in the sunlight, like Kory could reach out and touch chilled flesh.

"You're dead," she said. "Leave me alone."

Gerri's lips moved, forming words that Kory refused to hear.

Kory stepped around her and continued down the trail.

*

"It's flipping happening again." Barb, Kory's boss, a tall, athletic older woman who managed to make their dumpy forest service uniform look glamourous, stormed into their office and slammed a box of donuts down on their shared desk. "Three hikers saw ghosts this weekend."

Kory selected a raspberry filled donut, but regretted it when the red filling oozed out onto her hands. "I saw Gerri."

"Shit. I'm sorry, honey."

"You haven't called me honey since I was twelve years old."

Barb rolled her eyes. "Well, you haven't had to face your dead best friend's ghost since you were twelve, either."

"I'd happily pass on both experiences."

"Haven't you ever wondered what really happened? Maybe you could ask her."

Kory thought about that night fifteen years ago. About the rain and the ghosts and the sound of silent whispers. "No, I've never wondered."

51

*

The park was crowded again the next weekend, packed with people hoping to get a glimpse of the supernatural, or praying to get one last moment with lost loved ones, or planning to sell hot dots and shaved ice to the rubes.

Kory got herself a shaved ice and resigned herself to spending her day answering questions, which was hands down her least favorite part of her job.

Just after noon, she was considering a hot dog when Casper Wallace drove up. He was still driving the ancient Toyota Camry that they'd both lost their virginity in.

Kory hated that car.

Casper wasn't exactly dressed for the outdoors in his crisp khakis, untucked polo shirt, and sandals. He smiled and waved when he saw her, and headed straight over, pulling a tiny notebook out of his back pocket and grabbing the pencil that was tucked behind his ear. "Kory! Hi! I have some questions."

Kory plastered on her best customer service smile. "The closest restrooms are half a mile down the road, and the trail on the right is the one that leads to the lake."

"I want to talk to you about the ghosts."

"The park service has no official position on that matter."

He sighed. "Don't be like this."

"I'm on duty, Casper. Do you have any questions related to the park? Are you interested in renting a pavilion?"

"I want to know if the ghosts are affiliated with specific trees, or if they can appear anywhere in the woods."

Kory shrugged and glanced at his bare toes. "Then I suppose you should do some research."

Casper frowned at her again, then walked away.

But he was back in a few minutes, struggling to carry two hot dogs, two shaved ices, and two bottles of Pepsi.

Kory took pity on him and grabbed a hot dog before he could drop it. "Bribing a public official is a serious offence." He'd put ketchup and onions on the hot dog. Just the way she liked it. She sighed and relented. "I can draw you a map to where I saw her."

"You saw her?"

Kory nodded. "She's still wearing your shirt."

"Did she say anything?"

Kory shrugged. "Nothing I heard."

He took her sketched map and strode off into the woods.

Kory only half-hoped that he'd be bitten by a rattlesnake.

*

That night, Kory woke up standing in the woods in her bare feet and ratty pajamas. Gerri stood before her, glowing in the moonlight.

The summer night was warm, but Kory shivered anyway. "I told you to leave me alone," she said.

"It should have been you," Gerri said, her voice carried within the sound of the leaves, rustling in the breeze, and Kory had no choice but to listen, now. "You were the one they wanted. The one who could hear them."

"I told you it was dangerous. I told you to stay inside. It's not my fault that you didn't listen."

"They still want you," Gerri said.

"Even if you give me to them, you'll still be dead."

"I don't want to give you to them, you dick. I just want to talk. I died so you could live, and what are you doing with that gift? You're wasting it!"

"You may have died for me, but you still don't get to judge my life choices."

"All you do is hide in the woods."

"And that makes me happy."

"Does it? Tell me the truth."

"It really does. I like my job. I like my boss. I like being alone out here."

"What about Casper?"

Kory rolled her eyes. "I know you thought we were destined to be together, but it just didn't work out."

Gerri sighed. "He misses you, you know."

"That sounds like a him problem."

Gerri reached her hands out. "You're really happy?"

Kory's fingers passed through empty space when she reached back. "I am."

"And you don't want to take Casper back and have a baby girl and name her after me?"

"Not really. Sorry."

She sighed. "If you'd died, I'd totally have a baby and name her after you."

"That's very sweet of you."

She sighed again. "I could haunt you till you do what I want, you know."

"But you won't. Because you've always been the nice one."

"And look where that got me. Ugh. Fine. No haunting. I know you like being alone, but maybe come visit me sometimes?"

Kory nodded. "I promise."

Gerri vanished, and Kory was along among the trees.

Just the way she liked it.

Though, as she walked back over rocks and pine needles, she would have preferred to have her hiking boots.

Prompt #11
"Wholesome cult that goes wrong when they accidentally summon an evil unicorn."

I had so much fun writing this story. I'm looking including it in future readings, because I think it'll be a blast to perform.

Unicorn Dreams

For Courtney

Sunbeam gathered her rainbow-dyed hair back into an untidy ponytail and belted her silver, faux-fur lined robe at her waist. Obviously, she'd never wear real fur. Fur was Murder.

It was Monday, the Day of Worship. Though obviously, every day should be a Day of Worship, since every day was a Miracle that deserved Gratitude and Attention. But Monday was the day that she streamed new videos on YouTube, and the day that Indigo and Saffron didn't have to work at the convenience store or the hairdresser.

Sunbeam was above such mundane pastimes as a job—her videos brought in some money, and she got a few donations every month. Plus she'd inherited her grandmother's estate, which was a complete Blessing.

She entered her Studio. It had once been her grandmother's farm shed, but she'd done a lot of work to make the Aesthetic match her Aura. Tiny lights twinkled from every corner and along the walls and ceiling, veiled by brightly colored, gauzy scarves. One YouTube commenter said it was like she lived inside a Rainbow Cloud, which she Absolutely Loved. The floor was piled with pillows, where her Devoted Friends could recline.

Indigo was already in position, cradling her ukulele. Saffron was distributing beverages and snacks. All their offerings were GMO Free, Organic, and Whole. After all, you could only get Out of Life what you Put In. Processed sugar was a drug, and, as Sunbeam was always sure to remind her Faithful, Drugs Kill Dreams.

Sunbeam turned the camera on, then strode to her keyboard and played a welcoming chord. "Good morning, everyone!" She hopped up and down and clapped from the pure Joy that seeing her Devoted Friends gave her.

Saffron picked up her tambourine and gave it a happy shake. Indigo strummed her ukulele.

"I have a Super Special program planned for today! And hopefully, at the end, we'll have a Mystery Guest!"

Saffron and Indigo shot her alarmed looks. Her last Mystery Guest had been a ghost summoned through a Ouija board, who'd done nothing but spell out crude comments about Sunbeam's body. She'd since wondered if she'd tapped into a false spirit created by YouTube commenters instead of a true Ghost, but she hadn't tried again.

But this time, she had a better plan. She'd summon a Unicorn. A being of Purity and Light and Love.

She led her Devoted Friends through a few songs, till she could feel their Spiritual Energy flowing through room like warm honey.

She left the keyboard to Dance, gathering the Spiritual Energy into herself, careful not to leave the frame of the video. As the song ended, she let out a cry and reached her hands toward the ceiling, toward the sky beyond, toward the Shimmering Stars that hid behind the blue.

The Unicorn coalesced before her, growing from a single point of light. It was just as beautiful as she'd imagined. Its spiral horn shimmered with pearly iridescence, its dainty hooves glittered like stardust, and its white coat and mane glowed like the purest moonlight.

Her Devoted Friends gasped and clapped.

The Unicorn lowered its head, and Sunbeam reached out to touch its cheek.

The Unicorn lunged forward and speared its lovely horn straight into Sunbeam's chest.

HOW DARE YOU DISTURB MY DREAMS, The Unicorn thundered, its voice booming inside Sunbeam's mind. Through her pain and panic, she wondered if her YouTube audience would be able to hear its words.

"I'm sorry," Sunbeam said, her voice weak and wheezing. The Unicorn's horn pinned her in place as her lungs struggled to expand.

Up close, The Unicorn was even more Beautiful. Its eyes contained all of the Stars in the Heavens, concentrated in a single shining point. Sunbeam lifted a shaking hand and stroked its Velvety Nose. It was softer than anything she'd ever imagined.

I WILL DESTROY YOU FOR YOUR INSOLENCE.

Sunbeam knew she should feel Fear, but instead her Being was suffused with Awe. What a Blessing, to perish while Gazing Upon The Unicorn.

Indigo hit The Unicorn's beautifully arched neck with an old, rusty shovel that they'd hidden behind a plastic plant.

Sunbeam cried out in horror and shock. The Unicorn screamed in pain and rage.

"You leave her alone!" Saffron shouted, bringing her tambourine down on The Unicorn's head with a discordant crash.

The Unicorn reared, lifting Sunbeam's feet off the floor, then sending her flying through the air. The layers of scarves softened her impact with the sturdy wood wall.

Sunbeam clutched her chest, hoping to slow the flow of blood, but there was no wound, only a perfectly round scar that shimmered with the same pearly iridescence as The Unicorn's horn.

Her Devoted Friends surrounded the Cruel Beast. Some suffered kicks from its dainty hooves before they pinned it to the floor, panting on its side.

Sunbeam approached, feeling just a little dizzy from her impact with the wall. Her Devoted Friends parted before her, and she laid a hand on The Unicorn's cheek. "I Forgive You," she said. "And I Release you back to your Dreams."

The Unicorn flickered and vanished.

No one was seriously injured, which was a Miracle Beyond Reckoning. Sunbeam allowed each of her Devoted Friends to place a hand over her new, beautiful scar.

Eventually, the crowd left, and Sunbeam switched off the camera. She and Saffron and Indigo set to tidying the mess that the fight with the Unicorn had made. The snack table had overturned, spilling a half-full pot of fair-trade coffee, but most of the other food was salvageable. After all, what was the Ground but the World's Table?

"No more mystery guests," Indigo said.

Saffron nodded. "Seconded."

Sunbeam put a hand over her scar. It would have been a Glorious Death, but she was Grateful to be Alive. "No more Mystery Guests," she agreed.

They stood together and looked over their mangled snacks. Sunbeam wondered what The Unicorn Dreamed of.

"Let's go get donuts," she said.

Prompt #12
"Bird want shiny! Also, bird hate toes."

This was another fun one. Writing from the point of view of an animal is always a good time.

Charlie-Bird Saves Us All From the Alien Invaders, Or Bird Want Shiny

For Jojo T. Birbington

Charlie ruffled her feathers and edged sideways across her cage. The Keepers had been hasty in latching the door, and she could wriggle it open if she was quick and clever.

Charlie was always quick and clever. A *pop and snick* later, and she was fluttering to freedom.

The Keepers squawked their incomprehensible, tuneless song at each other. She stayed on the floor, since they were less likely to notice her if she kept from flying and flapping.

Of course, being on the floor put her in danger from their massive feet and their wretched claw-less toes. One of the Keepers insisted on painting the dull not-claws on the end of her toes the color of delicious berries. No rational creature could blame Charlie for pecking at them. Sometimes she forgot that they weren't berries. Other times, she was just angry that weren't berries. Either way, pecking was the clear solution. The other Keeper kept her feet tucked into fuzzy coverings that were often covered in alarming patterns.

Those, at least, helped Charlie avoid accidental kicks.

The Keeper's squawks grew louder and louder, and then the door to the mysterious outside splintered open. Two strange figures, both like the Keepers, but also horribly not, surged into the room.

Their limbs were long and spindly and their eyes huge in their thin, gray faces. They pointed a stick at the Keepers and squawked something even more discordant than the Keeper's usual sounds.

But the most interesting them about the intruders was the shiny thing attached to the middle of each of their foreheads. They caught the light in the most appealing way, and Charlie wanted them.

She more than wanted them. She needed them.

She launched herself from the floor, aiming straight at the first intruder's face. It squawked in fear and waved its arms wildly, but she had practice dodging the Keeper's attempts to capture her.

She grabbed the shiny thing with her beak and wrenched it off of the intruder's forehead.

It let out a horrific keening sound and fell to the ground.

The Keepers, following her fine example, tackled the second intruder and pulled the shiny thing off of its forehead.

Charlie dropped hers into the sunshine that fell through the splintered door. She pecked it a few times, admiring how the light glittered off of it.

The Keepers gave her the second shiny and called her, "Good Bird," which she knew was how they paid tribute to her. She preened under their warm attention. She flew to her favorite's shoulder and snuggled into her neck, crooning to indicate that she would also enjoy a snack.

The Keeper hurried to oblige her.

The Keepers did stuff her back into her cage, but they left the two shiny things and a pile of treats larger than she was before they hurried out, looking determined and hopeful.

Charlie hoped they brought back more shiny things. And treats.

Prompt #13
"A trip to Florida and a boat."

As luck would have it, I took a trip to Florida and stayed on a boat right before I wrote this, and I was really happy to get to set something in the Everglades.

At the End of Everything, There is the Sea

For Skip, from Vicky

He preferred spending his time in what had been parks or farms or ruins. Places that had always been empty of people, where space stretched out around him without any sign that the world had ended. Cities were choked with bones, small towns eerie in their silence and emptiness. But here, he could pretend that he was alone by choice, that he might encounter another hiker or explorer around any bend.

He'd been wandering south for a while now, and was pretty sure he was in the Everglades. He'd never been before, but the land around him matched the pictures his sister had sent back from her vacation. An unbroken expanse of yellow-green grass stretched out toward the horizon, swaying in the breeze. White, long-legged birds dotted the scene, and hints of water glinted in the hot sun. He stood calf-deep in muddy water, his pants rolled to his knees and his feet protected by a pair of hiking sandals that he'd liberated from an empty sporting good store.

He tried not to worry about leeches. Or alligators. Or where they crocodiles? He could never remember, and he didn't have a way to check. Not anymore.

He walked. His feet were cool, but sweat trickled down his neck, the backs of his knees, into his eyes. He wore a hat and a lightweight long-sleeved shirt to protect his skin from the relentless sun, but the back of his neck and tip of his nose pulsed with burning pain. He filled his canteen with brackish water and sipped it through a LifeStraw.

He walked, and he tried to appreciate the beauty that stretched out around him.

He walked, and tried not to think about his sister, smiling in her selfies, dying in his arms.

He walked, because what else was there for him to do?

And eventually, he couldn't walk anymore.

The ocean stretched out in front of him, blue and shining and endless. A boat bobbed in the waves to his left, tied to a decaying dock.

He allowed himself half an hour of hope. He called out a greeting, searched the boat for signs of recent life.

Of course there was no answer. Of course there were no signs. Of fucking course.

The boat was pretty, with blue-and-white painted sides, and when he climbed inside and down into its guts, he found himself surrounded by windows on all sides. Blue-tinted sunlight streamed past a school of darting fish. It was a tourism boat, then. Not a glass-bottomed one, though. After a few moments of thought, the name came to him, remembered from a glossy pamphlet. A semi-submarine.

The gas tank was full, and the engine spluttered to life after a few attempts. The steering was ungainly and he bumped the dock as he pulled away. But not hard enough to do any damage, so what did it matter? It wasn't like there was anyone around to judge his boat-driving skills.

He cruised for a while, then dropped anchor and went below. Fish darted in colorful reefs, and a manatee floated by, serene and stately. He ate a protein bar. He slept.

Sometimes, he wanted to just give up. Lie down and not bother getting up again. But most of the time, he felt like he had to keep himself alive for as long as possible, felt the weight of every previous generation of humanity pressing on his shoulders, felt responsible for seeing the species through one more day, one more hour. Because as far as he could tell, he was the last.

He was less lonely, out on the ocean, sitting in his boat with the water on all sides.

Eventually, he'd get sick or get hurt or run out of food.

Eventually, no matter what he did, he'd be gone, too.

But the sea would remain. And for what it was worth, that was some comfort.

Prompt #14
"Angels."

This was actually the very first story I wrote for this project. It's such a hopeful little thing, it felt like a good start.

Everyday Miracles

For Catherine Bussey

The Archangel Gabriel, since they existed as an extension of God's unconditional love, was incapable of feeling hatred. There was nothing in God's creation that they hated. But they were certainly not fond of rush hour traffic.

They glared at their phone, which kept informing them that they were still on the fastest route, and wished that the Archangel Uriel, whose turn it was to pick the restaurant, had selected one that wasn't quite so far out from the city center.

At times like these the Archangel Gabriel very much missed the days when they could fly about openly.

And smite things. They missed smiting things.

They often wondered why smiting things had fallen so far out of fashion. Surely, the Impala in front of them merited smiting. It had a vanity plate that read THKK-BO1. The Archangel Gabriel wasn't exactly sure what THKK-BO1 meant—they could know, if they wanted to, since all knowledge of God's creation was theirs for the asking. They preferred not to. But they were sure that it was obnoxious.

Traffic inched forward. THKK-BO1 cut into the left lane without using his turn signal. Then, after about 10 minutes, he merged back into the Archangel Gabriel's lane, again without signaling.

The Archangel Gabriel allowed him back in, because they were a literal angel.

They thought longingly of flaming swords.

Then, finally—finally—they arrived at their exit. From there it was only a short jaunt to the diner's parking lot, and the Archangel Gabriel had to admit that not having to drive around looking for street parking was a blessing.

The diner was a fairly typical example of its type. A little rundown, but the coffee smelled good. A model train track looped around the room on a high shelf clearly built for that purpose, which the Archangel Gabriel found charming. The Archangel Uriel waved from a booth in the corner, and the Archangel Gabriel glanced at the list of desserts scrawled on the whiteboard before joining them.

"Michael and Raphael are running late," the Archangel Uriel said as the Archangel Gabriel settled onto the worn green vinyl seat.

The Archangel Gabriel sighed. "Of course they are."

The waitress approached and gave the Archangel Gabriel a warm smile. "Hey there sugar, can I get you some coffee?"

The Archangel Gabriel nodded and gazed into the woman's soul. Julia Marie Davis, known as Jules to her friends. Thirty-four years old. She worked at the diner during the day, did medical transcription in the evenings, and was taking classes to become a master gardener on the weekends. She struggled to make ends meet, but was still sending money to help her niece through college. She liked flowers and spring rain and horror movies, and she loved the model train.

She turned to the Archangel Uriel. "Want me to warm yours up for you?" The Archangel Uriel nodded, so she topped off their cup with fresh coffee. "You're still waiting on two more, right?" The Archangel Uriel nodded again. "All righty then. You two just let me know if you need anything else while you wait."

The two archangels sat in silence, sipping their coffee. The Archangel Gabriel watched the model train complete two full circuits of the diner before the Archangel Michael and the Archangel Raphael strode in.

"I told them we needed to get moving a half hour earlier," the Archangel Raphael said. "But they never listen."

The Archangel Michael just rolled their eyes and slid into the booth next to the Archangel Gabriel.

"Looks like the gang's all here," Jules said. "Do you both want coffee? The menus are there on the table."

"We do want coffee," the Archangel Michael said. "What pies do you have today?"

"There's a list on the whiteboard," the Archangel Gabriel said. "It's right by the door."

The Archangel Michael rolled their eyes again. "I must have missed it."

"It's no trouble," Jules said, and recited the full list from memory.

The archangels ordered pie.

"We'll all be on separate checks, if that's not too much trouble," said the Archangel Raphael.

"Not at all," said Jules.

The archangels ate their pie and drank their coffee. The model train chugged along overhead.

"It's my turn to pick next week," the Archangel Raphael reminded them. "I have it narrowed down to two places, I'll text you when I make up my mind."

The Archangel Gabriel had their next twelve choices already selected. They liked to plan ahead.

After another coffee refill, Jules gave them each a bill for $4.62. "There's no rush at all," she said. "You all just take your time and let me know if I can get you anything else."

Each archangel pulled out a crisp $100 bill, then they left without asking for change. The Archangel Gabriel was sure that Jules would put the money to good use.

Prompt #15

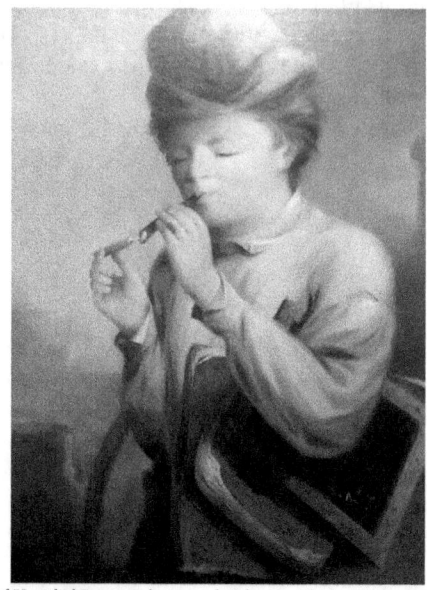

Photograph of Untitled Portrait by David Gilmour Blythe courtesy of Aimee Picchi

I got two picture prompts, and both were such delights. There's so much going on in this, it was really easy to get a story out of it.

Gunpowder Plot

For Aimee

"When you said we were going to blow up the patriarchy, I didn't think you meant tonight," Mary Ellen said, grasping the hem of her skirt as she crouched behind a hedge.

Patricia shrugged and held up another firecracker to her cigarillo, puffing as the wick hissed to sparking life. She didn't have a free hand, so her skirt trailed through the mud. Mary Ellen suspected that her new friend didn't care about stained hems.

Patricia threw the firecracker with practiced ease, and it exploded with a sharp bang.

"What if someone is injured?" Mary Ellen asked. "It's much more likely to be one of the servants than their master, you know."

"I've taken precautions." Patricia held her last remaining firecracker out to Mary Ellen, one eyebrow raised.

Mary Ellen took a deep breath and took it.

Patricia grinned around her cigarillo, and leaned forward, so Mary Ellen could light the firecracker. It almost slipped out of her shaking, sweaty hand when the wick started sparking, but she managed to toss it away, up and over the stone wall. This bang seemed more satisfying, somehow.

Mary Ellen just hoped that she was right to trust Patricia's precautions.

The sounds of men shouting and dogs barking reached their ears. Patricia stood, dropped her cigarillo into the mud, and strode toward the road, the very portrait of propriety. As long as you didn't notice the mud on her skirt, anyway. Mary Ellen hurried after her, still shaking.

*

Mary Ellen's brother paced back and forth across their front parlor. It was a largish space, so he could take a healthy number of steps before he twirled around. "Your fiancé's home was attacked last night."

"Oh no!" Mary Ellen said, feigning surprise as easily as breathing. "Was anyone injured?"

"He wasn't home."

"What about the servants?"

Her brother stopped and blinked at her. "Who cares?"

Mary Ellen did, but knew better than to say so. She could only hope that the servants hadn't been home, either.

Her brother went back to pacing. "The attack was the work of Feminists, using their infernal explosives. The damage was minor, but he no longer feels safe, and will be returning to his country estate."

Mary Ellen suppressed a grin. "I suppose that is wise."

"He wants you to accompany him."

"What? No. I refuse."

Her brother turned toward her, his eyes hot. "You should know better to gainsay me, Mary Ellen," he said. Flames flickered over his fingers as he stalked toward her.

He hadn't burned her since they were children. But that didn't stop him from threatening her.

Mary Ellen raised her chin, fighting down her fear. "You want him to marry me, not make me into his mistress. Do you think he would behave like a gentleman if you put me at his disposal?"

Her brother hesitated, possibly considering how he'd behave in such a situation, possibly considering her fiancé's past behavior. The fire in his hands spluttered and died. "Perhaps you are correct." He sighed. "I suppose we'll have to see about moving the wedding date up."

*

Patricia perched on the bed while Mary Ellen worked asbestos into her wedding veil. She arranged a series of vials, each filled with coarse gray powder, on the coverlet. "This was as much as I could get for you."

Mary Ellen pinned the veil to her hair and looked at reflection, pleased with the way the veil softened her features. "It'll be enough," she said.

"Are you sure he'll..." Patricia trailed off.

Mary Ellen looked down at the smooth scar that encircled her left wrist, the exact size and shape of her fiancé's hand. It was normally covered by an extravagant bracelet that he'd presented to her brother. "I'm sure," she said.

*

Mary Ellen knelt in the church and parroted words with no feeling behind them. Her brother, smug and resplendent in black silk, took her hand and gave it to the man who was now her husband.

Both of them held her hand so hard that their knuckles went white.

She could do nothing but endure. For now.

After the ceremony, there was feasting, then dancing. Her delicate glass shoes hurt her feet and did nothing to hide the blood when her blisters broke.

Her husband did not allow her to sit out a single dance.

Eventually, he scooped her into his arms and carried her to a waiting carriage, to the whoops and cheers of his friends and Mary Ellen's brother.

His breath against her ear was almost as hot as his hands. He left dark hand prints on pale silk.

He carried her again, out of the carriage, through the gate. Mary Ellen caught sight of some damaged stonework here and there, and she smiled, in spite of everything.

He dropped her onto the bed and turned away to undress.

She pulled off her shoes, wincing at the scrape of glass against raw skin. Blood pooled in the toebox, stained the soles of her feet crimson.

Her husband turned back, his grin savage, his hands already on fire.

Mary Ellen tossed her shoes toward him and rolled away, off the bed, her knees colliding with the floor, as he caught the shoes by reflex.

The powder concealed in the heels ignited, and they exploded in his hands.

His screamed echoed through the house. But no one came. Screams were expected, tonight.

Mary Ellen twisted her wedding veil around his still-burning hands, tossed specially prepared pitchers of water on the spreading fires, and waited, first for the screams, then the bleeding, to stop.

She found herself crying, and she wasn't sure why.

She limped down the stairs, leaving a trail of bloody footprints on the marble stairs. At the door, she took a slow, deep breath. Then she burst out onto the street, screaming about a horrible accident, begging for someone, anyone, to help her.

*

She wore black to the funeral. The papers all carried stories about the brave young widow, sole heir to her husband's vast estate. They didn't mention her new companion, who stood next to her and kept herself between Mary Ellen and her brother.

And if glass slippers were suddenly more popular as wedding shoes, well, no one with any influence paid any attention to the pointless whims of women's fashion.

Prompt #16
"Use your own idea."

We get a good number of foggy mornings in Pittsburgh, and one of them inspired this.

The Shape of Future Days

For Annette B. Maresh, from Dan

Wisps of fog clung to the ground around Alison's ankles as she walked across her driveway. She took a sip of still-too-hot coffee and dropped her keys as she struggled with the key fob.

A tendril of frost-cold fog wrapped around her wrist when she reached down to pick them up. She brushed it away, but it clung to her skin like insubstantial cotton candy. Then the morning sun crested the hill behind her house, and it burned away in an instant.

She took a deep breath. She told herself that she was imagining things. That it was nerves about going back to work, but all she felt was numb. And her wrist was still cold.

*

Her workday was long and stressful. Work had piled up during her bereavement leave, but she still wasn't ready to be back. None of her coworkers knew what to say to her. Conversations died when she entered the room.

Patty from HR hugged her, and she forced her face into something resembling a grateful smile.

She ate leftover casserole for dinner and ignored the half-empty bottle of red wine on the kitchen table.

*

The next morning, the fog was waist high. She almost expected resistance when she stepped into it, but it parted easily, swirling around her when she moved. The cold ate through her jeans, crept in above her socks. She kept a careful hold on her keys—she didn't want to have to bend into the fog to pick them up.

From inside her car, it was almost at eye level. Silvery shapes danced in the mist. A ghostly butterfly fluttered against the glass. Then the sun crested the trees, and it was gone.

*

She wasted her whole workday preparing for a presentation that had been moved up while she was gone, and had already happened. Her boss just patted her on the shoulder and offered to listen if she needed to talk.

There was only one person she wanted to talk to. But that person was gone.

That night, she finished the wine.

*

The next day, the fog was a solid wall, obscuring everything past her porch. The butterfly was back again, and a silvery tendril beckoned to her as she stood in her doorway. The fog dampened any sounds, but she felt the vibration of distant singing in the soles of her feet.

Alison reached one hand forward, and the tendril wrapped around her wrist again. Gentle and cold, it held without pulling. The butterfly landed on her outstretched palm. Its icy feet tickled.

The sun would be up soon. She could wait, she suspected that the fog wouldn't come again.

Her life wasn't bad, even now. It was her grief making each day pointless, and with time it would get better. Everyone said so.

She could see the shape of all of her future days, looming in front of her. Not bad, not great. Normal. Hollow.

There was no telling what would happen in the fog.

She stepped through the door.

Prompt #17

"The King of the Mushroom Forest" courtesy of Betsy Bodamer

I love this picture so much. It was just a joy to write a story inspired by it.

King of the Mushroom Forest

For Sylvi

The King of the Mushroom Forest proceeded through its domain like a glacier, slow and inexorable. Dew darkened the top of its glossy brown shell and dripped from the fungus and fern fronds that dotted its surface. Its graceful antlers arced over the tree-sized mushrooms, their silvery-gray surface ethereal and almost mist-like in the thin morning sunlight.

Its vast snail-like body should have left behind a trail, but the fragile spring flowers that peaked out of the leaf mold behind it were untouched, with not a single petal bruised.

Marta peered at it from behind a mossy boulder. Her fingers itched to sketch it, but she couldn't look away as the vast creature glided closer and closer.

She hadn't expected it to be so beautiful.

Its face swung toward her. Its deep brown eyes held surprising warmth and intelligence. It spotted her, and slowly turned its head as it passed, watching her. Weighing her.

Marta froze. It was slow, and even with its vast size, she didn't think it could pose a threat to her. Still, fear crept along her veins as it stared.

She met its eyes. The sky and earth and towering mushrooms all spun around her. She heard the sound of distant bells, smelled decomposing leaves and rain.

Then it looked away, and continued on its path, its slow, smooth pace uninterrupted.

When it was gone, she sketched frantically, trying to capture every detail.

That night, she dreamed she stood on top of its shell and they glided along together, fast enough that the wind stung tears from her eyes.

She woke with the sound of bells fading in her ears.

*

Marta's brother, Mica, frowned at the sign she'd painted for his new store. "I wasn't expecting the mushrooms," he said. "I thought it would just be the shop's name."

She'd painted tiny red-spotted mushrooms growing around the bottom of the sign. "We live next to a mushroom forest now," she said. "I thought it would be appropriate."

Mica sighed. "It's fine. I suppose I should be glad it isn't something more fanciful."

Marta traced one of the glossy painted mushrooms. She knew better than to expect gratitude from Mica, but his lack of appreciation for her work still stung.

"I'll get this hung up, you go organize the dry goods on the shelves."

Marta did as he asked. At least there was some joy in finding the perfect spot for everything, in displaying the goods just so. After hours of work, everything was finally set.

She wasn't sure where Mica had gone after hanging the sign, but she knew he'd want dinner when he got back, so she set to making it.

✻

They had their grand opening the next day. It went well. A few people even commented on how pretty the sign was, or how welcoming and orderly everything looked on the shelves, and Marta practically glowed with pride.

After the store closed for the day, she found herself wandering back toward the mushroom forest. She didn't see the King, but she felt welcomed and wanted as she settled down on a sturdy waist-high mushroom to sketch.

It was growing dark by the time she looked up.

Mica was waiting in their rooms behind the shop. "Where have you been?" he demanded. "I had a big day today, I want my dinner."

Marta didn't bother pointing out that she'd worked just as hard as he had—maybe harder, since she'd been in charge of taking money and fetching and carrying, while he chatted and shook hands. She didn't bother pointing out that he could have made dinner for himself instead of sitting around and waiting for her. She didn't bother saying anything at all. She just cooked his dinner.

✻

The next time she saw the King, snow dusted the top of its shell, and frost sparkled on its antlers. But it didn't seem bothered by the cold, its serene gliding pace was just as stately and slow over snow as it had been over mud and fallen leaves and flowers.

But this time, when it looked at her, it stopped.

82

It spoke to her, not in words, but in a cascade of images and feelings and tastes.

It asked why she was so sad.

No one had ever asked her that before.

It was strange to see it motionless, so she walked with it, one hand against its smooth, cold shell. Distant bells chimed in her ears as she poured out her whole story. Her parents gone, her brother unappreciative, her own dreams distant and impossible.

The King of the Mushroom Forest listened, and cared, and considered. It could do little to help, because the realms of men were beyond its reach.

But it could listen, and maybe that was enough.

Perhaps she could get her brother to listen to her, too. And if Mica turned her out, the King would make sure she had shelter in the forest.

As she walked home to ask for what she needed, she could hear distant bells over the snow crunching beneath her boots, and she knew that she wasn't alone.

Prompt #18
"Story of a huntress witch! Maybe she uses a bow and arrow."

This is another story that is set in the same world as *The Forest God*.
Coming up with another magical element for to add to the mythology of
the world was great fun.

The Huntress

For Laine

A Huntress is only born when there will be need for her, which is fortunate, for her birth is a cruel thing. Her mother will find herself called to the woods under a full moon, will wander from her warm bed and safe house, eyes closed and feet bare, deep into the heart of the forest.

There, the Huntress will be born. Her hair silver, her eyes dark as the midnight sky, her tiny hands grasping. The forest's Witch will take the child in, and the Forest God will guard the mother till morning, when she will wake to her loss.

The Huntress will pass from forest to forest, from Witch to Witch. She is attached to no place, is bound by no entangling affection. She serves the Moon, and must be as just and as cold as her celestial mistress.

*

The Huntress glowered at the apprentice Witch. The girl still had a name, but the Huntress refused to learn it. Why bother, when the girl would just give it up when she became a full Witch?

It wasn't like the two of them could ever be friends.

The Huntress could have no friends.

"I want you to teach me how to shoot a bow," the apprentice Witch said. "You're good at it, right?"

The Huntress could pierce the eye of a songbird from half a mile away. But she had never had to learn. She simply understood how to use her bow the instant she touched it. "I am the best," she said. "But I am not sure I can teach you."

"Why not? I promise I'll work hard. I'm no shirker."

The Huntress sighed. "Fine. I will try."

*

A Huntress is only born when there will be need for her. As each Huntress grows, so does the threat that she was born to face. A monster, outside the balance. Sometimes it is a Dragon, its egg stolen from its mother,

85

twisted into a creature of greed and caprice. Sometimes it is something new, a creature with too many heads or limbs, born from a volcano or the bottom of the sea, its heart blackened by hate and rage before it even draws its first breath. Sometimes it is a Forest God that failed to protect its lands, then turned to darkness and revenge instead of fading away.

The Moon sees all, and sends her servants to restore the balance.

No Huntress has ever failed in her mission.

No Huntress has ever survived the fall of her enemy.

*

The apprentice Witch cried when the Huntress left. "I'll never see you again, will it?" she asked, her voice thick with tears.

The Huntress looked away from this unseemly display, shifted her weight from one foot to the other, then back again. "I will face my enemy soon," she said, ignoring the tight feeling in her own throat. "I feel it stirring in my dreams."

"Be careful," the apprentice Witch said.

"I will not," said the Huntress. "I must not. Goodbye."

As she turned away, the apprentice Witch reached out, pressed something small and soft into her hand. "It is a charm," the apprentice Witch said. "It will give you sweet dreams."

"I have no need for such a thing," the Huntress said. Still, she tucked it into her pocket.

No one had ever given her a gift before.

*

This time, the enemy was a creature born of nightmares. It stalked the Huntress through her dreams, but the blessing of the Moon protected her.

The Huntress stalked the monster in her waking hours, and it had nothing to protect it.

The monster wore a hundred faces. Her mother, the first Witch who found her in the woods, the Witch who gave her her very first bow. The apprentice Witch, who'd cried when they parted.

The Huntress did not hesitate. She loosed arrow after arrow, piercing hearts and throats and eyes. But the battle was exhausting, and the Moon's protection was at its weakest with the sun high overhead.

As she loosed her final arrow, the one that would sink deep into the monster's tiny, twisted heart, it dragged her mind into its nightmares, and her body fell, empty and lifeless.

The monster was dead, and the Huntress lost.

All was as it should be.

*

The apprentice Witch found the Huntress's body, lifeless and still. She found the monster, next to her, twisted and dead. The Huntress clutched her bow in one hand. But in the other, she held a small, soft charm.

The apprentice Witch took the Huntress's bow, because she could use it.

But she left the charm, because it had already served its purpose.

*

The Huntress expected to be trapped in an eternal nightmare, to be hunted for eternity by a monster that could wear any face.

But her dreams were warm and soft, full of long spring days and sunshine and soft, cool rain, perfect for dancing in. The apprentice Witch was there, and the Huntress knew her name.

And somehow, the apprentice Witch knew the Huntress's name as well. The one she'd only dared think of in her quietest thoughts, the one she'd given herself.

They danced together, in the Huntress's endless dream, laughing and spinning and happy.

Prompt #19
"Something spooky, of course!!!! I would also love it if the protagonist could be a badass female named River."

I don't often do urban fantasy, but I always enjoy it when I do.

Vampires, Dirty Alleys, and Black Cats that Aren't

For River

River leaned against a crumbling wall outside a rundown theater, waiting for the show to wrap up. She'd heard that the new star ducked out this door as soon as the applause stopped.

She was cold in her thin leather jacket, but managed to keep herself from shivering through sheer force of will.

The orange-tinted sodium streetlight at the end of the alley flickered and buzzed, and the cold autumn wind sent stray bits of trash swirling along the pavement. The alley smelled like old urine and new blood.

A small shadow detached itself from the general gloom and sauntered over to her. "Fancy seeing you here," it said.

River glared down at the black cat. She usually loved cats. But this wasn't really a cat. It was a spirit, and an annoying one at that. "What do you want?"

"Just checking in on my favorite monster hunter. I'm pleased to see that you're on the case."

"I don't work for you."

The spirit twined around her ankles. Its touch was like ice, even through her boots and thick socks. "I care little for whose orders you follow. I am only concerned with results, and I don't like it when beings under my protection are targeted."

"I hear the theater has a new leading lady."

"And you think that she's connected to the recent rash of disappearances?"

River shrugged. "The timing is suspicious."

The theater door opened, and a woman slipped out. She was bundled in a bright red faux-fur coat that was bright even in the flickering sodium light. Her hair was long and dark, her eyes large and dark, her lips full and dark. Her skin was unnaturally pale, like cream or porcelain. It seemed impossible that she could be a creature of flesh and blood. She was too beautiful, too delicate, too ethereal.

But she smelled human, without any hint of the grave rot of a ghoul or old dust of a vampire.

She let out a tiny yelp of surprise when she spotted River. She put one hand over her heart and clutched her purse close to her with the other. "You startled me. Who are you, and what are you doing here?"

Her voice was rich and velvety, deeper than River expected. "Are you Christina Martin?"

"I am." Her eyes flicked from River to the spirit, then back again. "People will come if I scream, you know."

"I'm not here to hurt you."

"You'll excuse me if I don't trust you, scary stranger. You seem to have an awful lot of knives."

"River."

"What about the river?"

"My name. It's River."

The spirit leapt and landed softly on River's shoulder. "As entertaining as this is, something is coming."

Another shadow coalesced into a human form. A man this time, again with the dark hair and eyes and pale skin. And this one did stink of old dust.

River drew her silver daggers. Christina Martin pulled an ornate silver cross out of her bag and held it like she meant to club the vampire with it.

"Oh, put that silly thing away," the vampire purred, his attention fixed on Christina. "You know I'd never hurt you."

"I know no such thing," Christina said. "I told you to leave me alone."

"You know I can't do that. I love you too much."

"I'm pretty sure love means listening when someone says no," River said, twirling her daggers so they flashed in the orange light.

"Consent is important," the spirit agreed, hopping back down from River's shoulder. "Even I know that."

"Just look at her," the vampire said. "She's obviously destined to be a vampire. Hers is just the kind of beauty that should last forever."

"I really should go get a spray tan," Christina grumbled.

The vampire gasped. "You wouldn't!"

While the monster was distracted, River struck.

Her dagger bit deep into the vampire's neck, but it twisted away from her at the last moment, and the wound closed in seconds.

"Your new friend is very rude," the vampire said. "Please tell her that we're having a private conversation."

"We aren't having a conversation at all," Christina said. "I told you I never wanted to see you again."

River jabbed forward, and the vampire dodged. "You didn't mean that," it said. "You couldn't. We're destined to be together forever."

"You're not destined for anything forever," River said. "You're not going to leave this alley."

The vampire rolled his eyes. "I'm going to kill you and feast on your blood, and then my darling Christina will finally listen to reason and become mine forever."

Christina brought the cross down onto the vampire's back. "I've told you a thousand times, that's never going to happen!"

River's daggers flashed, and the vampire's head bounced on the pavement. The shadows grew and stretched, and the body sank into them.

The spirit purred. "What a delicious treat. Thank you, River."

"I don't work for you," River muttered.

"I know, I know." It vanished back into the shadows. "That just means that I don't have to pay you, you know."

Christina leaned back against the theater door, shaking. "I didn't think he'd follow me here," she said. "Did he hurt anyone?"

River shrugged. "He was a vampire."

Christina winced. "That's a yes, then."

"He still would have hurt people, even if he hadn't followed you."

"Different people, though."

"Maybe. But you helped me stop him. He can't hurt anyone else, now."

That made her smile. She had a very pretty smile—it was crooked, and very human. "I guess that's something. Thanks, River."

A shadow wrapped around Christina's ankle as she stepped forward, and she tripped into River's arms. She was warm, and she smelled like cinnamon and oranges.

River managed not to blush through sheer force of will. "You're welcome. Come on, I'll walk you home."

Prompt #20
"A story about a bumbling Headless Horseman."

This was another fun prompt. I really got so many wonderful prompts through this project. My very favorite thing about this story is the main character's name.

Restitution

For Nathan

Josiah materialized above his grave as the last rays of autumn sunlight faded from the western sky. He crossed his spectral arms over his ghostly chest and shivered. He hated the dark, he hated the cold, he hated being a ghost.

Petunia, his self-appointed boss, floated over from her gaudy mausoleum. "It's your turn to terrorize the mortals," she said, tapping one finger on her clipboard.

Josiah hated clipboards. They hadn't existed when he was alive, and he was half convinced that Petunia had made them up just to make herself look important.

"Can't Gary do it? He actually enjoys it, and he's good at it."

"Nobody likes a shirker, Josiah."

In life, Josiah had worked incredibly hard. Plowing, sowing, reaping. He'd done everything that was ever expected of him. But instead of going on to some eternal reward, he was trapped in this cemetery. And if that wasn't bad enough, after a few centuries Petunia showed up and decided they needed structure.

Petunia threw up her hands. "It's not like I can make you do anything, Josiah God-Grant-Us-Patience White. But if you don't work, you don't get paid."

Josiah hated when she used his full name. He wished that time had eroded the letters on his tombstone before she could read them.

He had been dead for a long time. And even when he was freshly dead, his family hadn't been the type to do something as frivolous as putting flowers on his grave. They hadn't even bothered to plant a rosebush, which was all he'd really wanted.

And Petunia was the only ghost who still got remembrances from the land of the living. Her terrible mausoleum always had a fresh flower wreath on the door. And she'd share the energy from those remembrances, if you did what she wanted.

The energy was like early morning sunshine, warm and soft and golden.

It was the only thing about being dead that Josiah didn't hate. He sighed. "Fine. I'll do my best."

Petunia grinned at him. "Excellent. I have a costume idea for you."

*

Josiah had never really liked horses, not even before one threw him off and he broke his neck. He'd never shared that detail with Petunia, so he didn't think that she'd brought forth the huge black steed that was currently chomping on the grass on his grave out of malice.

It was a beautiful creature, with a coat as black as the midnight sky, and eyes that glinted like distant fires. Josiah hated it instantly. He also hated the billowing black robe and glowing jack-o-lantern that Petunia thrust into his arms.

"There, even you should be able to terrorize some mortals with this!"

Josiah was too exhausted to be terrorized, but he was pretty sure he'd be the only one suffering through this night. Still, he thought of the warm-light-feeling of the remembrances, climbed into the absurd robe and floated up onto the horse's back.

Petunia actually clapped. "You look great! Remember to hold the jack-o-lantern over your face, so the mortals will think it's your head! Then you can throw it at them!"

Josiah wished he'd never been born.

He rode a circuit around the cemetery. The horse beneath him and pumpkin clutched in his arms were actually warm, which was a pleasant surprise.

Maybe no one would trespass tonight, and he could just enjoy some peace and quiet. The night was dark and cold, with a bitter wind and thick clouds skuttling quickly across the sickle moon. If he was a mortal with any sense, he'd be safely at home with a fire and a good book.

Of course, he should have known that mortals don't have any sense.

He heard jeering ahead. A crowd of young voices, all aimed at one lone figure, standing apart. They were outside the fence, beyond his reach. But the lone figure approached the wrought iron barrier, looking back over their shoulder, as if hoping the rest of the mortals would conveniently vanish.

"Go on! You're not afraid, are you?"

The lone figure struggled over the fence, slipping and nearly falling no less than five times. But eventually, they landed hard on the ground, inside the cemetery.

Josiah approached, holding the jack-o-lantern in front of his face.

He hadn't expected the crowd outside to be able to see him. But if the screaming was any indication, apparently they could. They broke and ran, leaving Josiah alone with the trespasser.

"Are you going to kill me?" the trespasser asked, their voice resigned.

Josiah lowered the pumpkin so he could look at the trespasser properly. They were stout and short, with oddly-cropped hair, and wearing modern clothes that he would never understand. Couldn't these people tell that they looked ridiculous? Why did none of them even seem to own a hat? Had the art of hat-making been lost? He'd been buried without a hat, and he still felt its lack keenly.

He couldn't tell if the child was a boy or girl, but he supposed that didn't matter. They were trespassing, so should be terrorized. "Don't be absurd, I'm no murderer," he said. Which wasn't right at all, he should have laughed menacingly or something. "Still, you should not be trespassing in the cemetery at night."

The trespasser chewed on a thumbnail, which was an appalling habit that Josiah's own mother had often slapped him for as a child.

"Perhaps I could offer some restitution for my trespass?"

Restitution sounded promising. Very promising. "Do you know how to plant a rosebush?"

"It's not exactly rocket science, is it? Did a hole, put a plant in."

Josiah dismounted and held out the glowing jack-o-lantern. "I'm unfamiliar with rocket science, but I do think you have the basics of it. If you do this for me, not only will I let you go, but I will give you this to show your tormentors. You can tell them whatever story you wish. All I ask is that you plant a rosebush on my grave. My name is Josiah God-Grant-Us-Patience White. The letters are faint, but still legible."

"That's quite a name."

"I could still punish you instead of accepting your restitution."

The trespasser snatched the jack-o-lantern and hugged it close to their chest. "A rosebush. Got it."

"Very well." Josiah turned to float back onto the horse.

"Wait!" the trespasser called.

"What now?"

"Could you maybe help me to get back out of here? I'm not great at climbing."

Josiah gave the trespasser a boost, and the rest of the night passed without incident.

*

When Josiah materialized the next night, there was a rosebush planted on his grave. The colors were hard to see in the fading light, but he guessed they were pumpkin-orange. Which seemed an odd color for a rose, but the modern world was a strange place.

There were some other flowers planted, too. Mums and some unknown bulbs, almost vibrating with potential, and not just on his grave, but on all the neighboring ones, as well.

Maybe kids these days were all right, after all.

Warm energy washed over him, and Petunia nearly dropped her clipboard when she came by.

And for the first time since his death, Josiah felt truly happy.

Prompt #21
"A weird guided meditation."

I actually gave myself this prompt, because I have been trying out different meditations and so many of them are just bizarre. So I took that just a few steps farther.

Unravelling, a Guided Meditation

For All of You

Let's begin by taking a few slow deep breaths. In through your nose, out through your mouth.

Deep breath in.

Deep breath out.

Deep breath in.

Deep breath out.

You're doing great.

Now, let's start our body scan. Breathe in, and become aware of the soles of your feet. How they press against the floor. If they are warm or cold or neither. Slowly move your awareness up to your ankles, to the intricate puzzle of bones that fit together there. One of them is shaped like a key, and when your awareness brushes it, your whole body vibrates like a piano wire struck by a raindrop.

Move your awareness up your legs, to your calves. Your knees. Your thighs. Noticing any tightness, any silverfish-quick creatures weaving in and out between your muscle fibers, any aches or pains.

Move your awareness to your core. Feel how your body expands as you breathe in, how it contracts when you breath out. Feel the darkness pooling in the spaces between your organs. Feel the twisting thing that lives deep inside your heart, waiting and watching.

Now turn your attention to your arms. Your elbows. Your hands. Feel the strength in your fingers. Feel the strength in the space between your fingers.

Breathe in.

Breathe out.

Think about your skin, how thin and fragile it is, how it is your only barrier, your sole protection from the world that is constantly pressing in all around you.

Think about how all of you, every bit, including that protective layer of skin, is more space than matter.

You are your atoms.

You are the space between your atoms.

Hold onto that space. It is yours. Don't let the forces that push at you take it away.

Breathe in.

Breathe out.

You're doing great.

Think about a thing that is true, but you hate. Maybe it's the inevitability of your own death. Maybe it's an atrocity committed by your ancestors. Maybe it's that you are unable to fly through sheer force of will.

Breathe in.

Breathe out.

Imagine a door.

If that door opens, that true thing that you hate will unravel. It will no longer be true. The world will be different.

Think of all of the things that would change. The ripples of effect that the change would have on you. On your family. On the world.

The door is locked, of course.

But you have the key.

It's right there, in your ankle. Where it's always been.

Take it out. Don't worry, your other ankle bones will shift around its empty space, like it was never there.

The vibration is stronger now.

Take a deep breath, in through your nose.

And out through your mouth.

Put the key in the door.

Feel how it fits with a satisfying click.

Feel the vibrating stop, leaving you hollow and thin, like you're not quite real. Like you're a chalk drawing on a busy sidewalk, waiting for the rain.

Breathe in. You're still here.

Breathe out. You are your atoms. You are the space between your atoms.

Breathe in. Will you turn the key and open the door?

Breathe out. Or will you leave it closed and walk away, the soles of your feet pressed to the ground, the bones in your ankles shifting, then settling.

Breathe in.

Breathe out.

Make your choice.

Prompt #22
"Waiting."

This one is another self-prompt, and might be the shortest story I wrote for this project. I wrote it on my deck in early November 2020, and I'm sure you can guess what inspired it.

A Single Page Rescued from a Lady's Journal

For Amy and Betsy

We are too far from the front to hear or see or even smell signs of the battle. By all seeming, it is a normal day. A lovely one, at that. The sun is warm, the air cool. The breeze carries with it the scent of apples, heavy on their trees.

We do not know when to expect word. Perhaps there will be no word, only a first glimpse of an approaching army, sun glinting on freshly-blooded swords.

I should not be so morbid. But fear worries at the edges of my mind, eroding my ability to truly focus on anything. At any moment, we could be safe. At any moment, our world could shatter.

And we can do nothing but wait. We fill our time with everyday tasks. But what is the point of checking on the laundry when we could all be dead tomorrow? I am not alone in my distraction. None of us are much focused on our tasks.

I wish I was one of those warrior women that they speak of in tales. At least then there would be something I could do. Some way I could contribute. I have heard managing a household compared to managing an army. Perhaps I could have been a general, making decisions that matter, seeing results as they unfold. Or perhaps I could have been a sorceress, throwing lightning bolts at our enemies.

But I am not. I'm just me.

And I can do nothing but wait.

Prompt #23
"Santa retiring and passing the family duties to his daughter."

I love Christmas, and writing Christmas stories is always fun.

A Christmas Legacy

For Nathan

Kristina Kringle performed her first Christmas miracle when she was twelve. Her mother asked for some water, and when Kris turned on the tap, piping hot peppermint cocoa flowed out instead.

Her mom had been so proud and excited and relieved. The mantle of Santa had been handed down in their family for generations beyond counting, but never to a girl before, and Kris knew that her mother had been worried.

Kris had sipped her perfect peppermint cocoa and tried not to feel sick.

*

Christmas magic was an honor, a privilege, a gift.

It didn't matter that Kris had no interest in at all. It wasn't something she could return or pass along to someone who wanted it.

When she was sixteen, her father cleared a week of his busy schedule and took her camping. Kris couldn't remember the last time the two of them had spent much time together. She tried to act excited and hide the dread that sat heavy in the pit of her stomach.

She forced a smile and hummed Christmas carols as she strapped on her snowshoes and loaded her pack onto Dancer, her favorite of the reindeer.

The weather was cold, like always, but the low-lying sun cast a pretty sort of light, and the air was still. The snow crunching underfoot and the reindeer's occasional grumbling were the only sounds. The air around them smelled of fresh pine and gingerbread. Kris tried to enjoy the hike and not worry too much about whatever lectures or lessons her father had in store for her.

"I was never worried," her father said, breaking the long silence.

"Worried about what?"

"The Christmas magic. I always knew you'd have it. I saw the twinkle in your eye the first time I held you."

"You could have told Mom."

He shrugged. "I did. But you know how she frets."

Her father didn't look like the Santa Claus in stories. He was a big man, but more muscle than fat, and his hair and close-cropped beard were dark and just frosted with gray. His eyes did twinkle, though. That much was true. And the Christmas magic ensured that anyone who spotted him saw exactly what they expected to see.

The same would be true for Kris, if she ever took over.

When she took over. It was her destiny, after all.

She hated the thought of vanishing into Santa. Of being a role instead of a person.

They reached a spot that looked just like a dozen others they'd walked past, but her father stopped. "We're here."

They set up the tents and made a fire and sat next to it roasting marshmallows.

"I know you don't want to do it," her father said.

Kris flinched. "How?" She'd never breathed a single protest.

"Because I didn't want to do it, either. And neither did my father."

"But I will eventually?"

He shrugged. "I can't tell you how you'll feel in the future. But I can tell you that eventually, I was ready." He offered a marshmallow to Dasher, who sniffed it delicately then snorted and turned back to her hay. "It took me a century, though. We don't age like normal people. I can keep on being Santa till you're ready, no matter how long it takes."

"What if I'm never ready?"

He shrugged. "Then you never take over."

Kris's breath rushed out of her and a feeling of relief spread through her chest. "It won't break anything? I won't ruin Christmas?"

Her father laughed. "Absolutely not."

"What will I do instead? What did you do?"

"I travelled the world. Drove racecars. Sailed across the Atlantic Ocean. Spent a year in the Yucatan. You can do whatever you want. Your mother has family that you can stay with, to start. You can go to school, get a job. Don't get a job." He shrugged again. "And eventually, when you're ready, you can come back."

"Can I come back before I'm ready? To visit?"

"Of course," her father said. "It wouldn't be Christmas without you." He passed her a flask, and she took a sip of perfect peppermint cocoa, and found that she couldn't stop smiling.

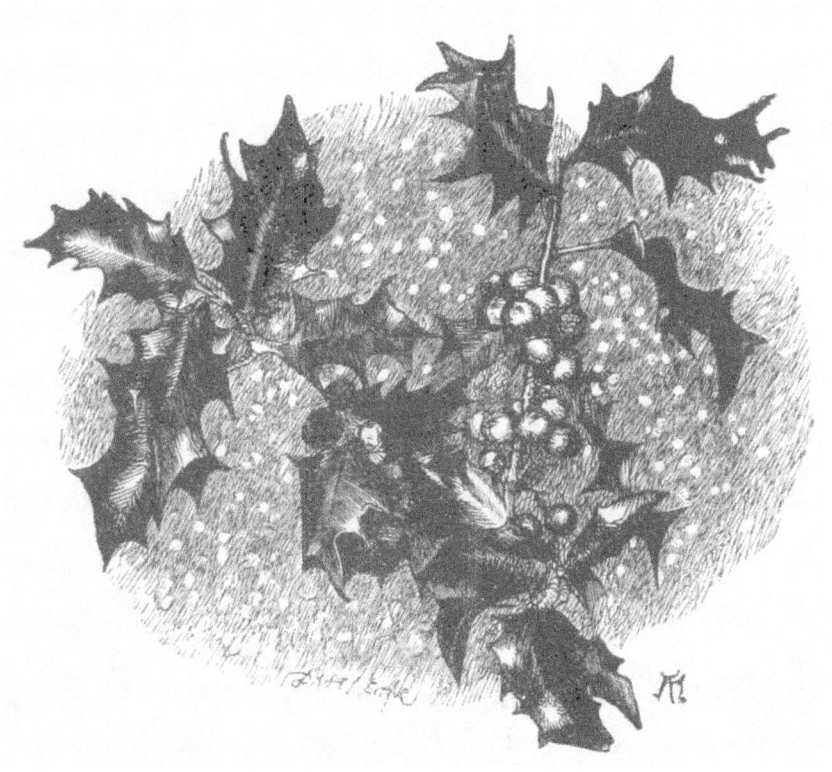

Prompt #24
"A happy Celtic story about new life in midwinter."

It feels wonderful to round out the year, and the project, with a happy story.

A Midwinter Miracle

For Shannon

Snow stretched in an unbroken expanse almost as far as Edan could see through their small window. It was beautiful and blinding in the morning sunshine. It was also a problem.

Lynette moved about behind him, tending to the fire and seeing to their breakfast.

"You should let me do that," Edan said, turning to her. She'd taken to wearing his clothes as her belly grew, but now even his shirts barely stretched to cover the swell of their unborn child.

"I prefer my breakfast unburnt." She shuffled sideways, scooping porridge into a bowl, somehow both ungainly and graceful.

Edan scowled at her. "I don't burn everything."

"No. I suppose not. Sometimes things are raw."

Then she let out a sudden, surprised sound and dropped her bowl. Edan lunged forward and just managed to catch it before it crashed to the floor.

Lynette lowered herself onto their bed, her hands pressed against her belly. "I think it's starting."

The snow was waist-high, at least. And their holding was a good five miles out of town. Edan fought down a wave of panic. "I don't think I'll be able to fetch the midwife in time. But I can try."

"No, stay. Please."

"We need a midwife."

"It'll be fine."

"I knew we should have gone to stay with your sister."

"You don't like my sister."

"I'd have learned to like her, if it meant keeping you safe."

"I don't really like her, either."

"How are you so calm?"

She shrugged. "Hand me the little box that I keep next to the honey. Then go put some snow in a pot and melt it. We'll need hot water."

Edan had never looked at the small wooden box that his wife kept next to the honey. It was carved with rowan berries and graceful fish, and when Lynette opened it, there was a single apple blossom inside, fresh as the day it bloomed. She whispered something into its delicate pink petals, then glanced up at him. "The water, my love?"

It took his full strength to even shift the door. There would be no help for them. And in spite of Lynette's calm, he couldn't help but feel afraid. This was their first child, neither of them really knew what they were doing.

When he turned back to his wife, clutching a pot full of snow, there was another woman leaning over her, moving pillows around to make her comfortable.

The woman wore a blue cloak that flowed like a river, eddying and swirling around her as she moved. Her features seemed plain and unremarkable, but they refused to stay in his memory when he glanced away from her.

"How did you get here?" he asked.

The woman smiled. "My daughter needed my help, so I am here."

"Who are you?"

"Who do you think I am, husband of my daughter?"

His guess felt absurd. But she'd appeared out of nowhere. Outside, the snow was still unbroken, unmarred by even the lightest footprints. "Danu?"

"The very same," the river goddess said. "Now, go get that over the fire. I will need it soon."

Edan spent the next hours doing whatever Danu requested. He boiled water, handed her rags, let his wife squeeze his hand.

His fear was gone, replaced by a slow-growing joy.

"Is the goddess your literal mother?" he asked his wife, keeping his voice low. "Or is it more of an adoption situation? Is our baby a quarter god?"

Lynette huffed a laugh between her contractions. "Do I seem like I am part goddess to you?"

"Yes?"

Lynette squeezed his hand.

"I'm already much fonder of your mother than I am of your sister."

"It's time," Danu said. "Push."

The next few minutes were a blur. Lynette screamed and pushed and held his hand in a crushing grip. Then Danu pulled their baby into the world and pressed a kiss to his red forehead before passing him to Lynette's waiting arms.

Edan gazed at his family in awe.

When he turned to offer Danu his thanks, she was gone.

"I never got my breakfast," Lynette said as she held the baby to her breast.

The bowl he'd saved from the floor was cold, and the porridge left in the pot was a blackened mess.

But there were two new bowls of porridge sitting by the fire, both perfectly cooked and still piping hot.

Edan handed one to his wife and gave silent thanks to his mother-in-law. For everything.

Bonus Story 1

I almost never write by hand anymore. I type much faster. But I wrote this story sitting by a fountain in Kansas City while I was at a writing convention.

Down the River

Trisha sits on the riverbank, on large, smooth stones that press cold against her thighs. She sits and watches the leaves swirl downstream. Brown, green, red, orange, yellow, all clumped together and flowing down the gray river.

The water is loud, running unchecked over rocks and branches. A few clumps of leaves catch and clog between the rocks, but not for long.

Never for long.

A single leaf, silver-green and narrow like a blade, catches on a lacy snag of ice that reaches, delicate and clear, out from the shore.

Trisha leans forward, plucks the leaf from the frigid water.

Her fingers tingle from the cold.

A scene plays on the backs of her eyelids. A hot day, a picnic basket overflowing with sandwiches and chips and lemonade in slender glass bottles. A breeze, whispering through green leaves overhead that are just leaves, just the part of the tree that breathes. Their shadows dance over skin.

The memory fades, but the taste of lemonade lingers on her tongue.

She is alone again, watching leaves that are no longer just leaves.

She should let this one go. It isn't the one she is searching for. It isn't for her.

Still, she holds the leaf between numb fingertips, careful not to bruise it.

The leaf trembles, impatient to be on its way.

She tucks it into her worn notebook, between pages filled to bursting with her own cramped handwriting.

The cold wind swirls around her, angry at her theft.

But she is not a leaf, and the wind cannot move her.

She clutches her notebook to her chest, wishing that there was a way for her to change the leaves inside it back into people.

Or that she could find a way to change herself into a leaf. At least then she wouldn't be alone.

She sits by the river and watches the leaves swirl downstream. There are so many of them.

So many, and she may have missed him already.

Time passes, and another leaf drifts into her reach. She holds it, listening and watching, then tucks it into her notebook. The wind protests again, and she smiles at it.

Keeping the wrong ones is still better than being alone.

Bonus Story 2

I know I wrote this for a very specific prompt, but to be honest I have no idea what it was, now. This one turned out a bit dark.

Home Fires

"Let us help," the women said as the generals' army approached. But their men just kissed their foreheads. "You wouldn't be any use in the upcoming battle," they said. "You can't fight. Just keep the home fires burning." So the women scrubbed the floors and simmered the stews and mended the shirts and waited.

After the battle was lost, when the army marched into their city, the women stood with heads bowed, their tired hands clasped before them.

The generals examined each woman. Most were left untroubled, released back to their cooking and sewing and scrubbing. But each general picked a woman to be his concubine in the beautiful palace their mages built for them in the very center of the city.

The remaining men sneered at the concubines, called them traitors and worse.

But they vanished behind ivory walls, and the men soon forgot about them.

The concubines snuck out of the palace when they could, carrying information along with their bruises. "Let us help," they said. "We have a plan."

The other women listened.

In the middle of the hot, dry season, the women sent their men away. "We have women's work to do," they said. "Go and farm or hunt or trade."

Then the women took the coals from their hearth fires and scattered them. In the dry heat, even the air seemed to catch.

Their home fires burned, and burned, and burned, leaving only ashes behind.

Bonus Story 3

I have no idea where this one even came from. I'm sure the prompt had something to do with space.

A Leveraged Buyout

Astrobotany wasn't a typical dream career, but Rowena couldn't remember wanting to do anything else. She reminded herself of that every time the station's mayor burst into her zero G greenhouse with a new demand.

Of course, his demands kept her from getting any work done. Still, he was her boss. She looked up from her tomato vines and fought to keep her expression friendly.

He didn't venture into the open space of the greenhouse, opting to cling to the handholds in the doorway. "The chef needs lemons to make mayonnaise."

"Lemons grow on trees, and trees take years to grow."

"I thought maybe they'd grow faster in space?"

The mayor's uncle was the major shareholder in the company that funded the station. He wasn't a scientist. Rowena doubted that he'd ever passed a science class.

"They don't," she said.

"Well, he said vinegar would do in a pinch. I'm counting on you!" He spun around and floated away, leaving Rowena to stare after him in dismay.

*

Rowena found Kristen, the team's microbiologist, running on a treadmill in the spinning section. "I need help," Rowena said. "The mayor wants vinegar."

"That man is disaster and mayhem," Kristen said between gasping breaths. "He should have been drowned as an infant."

"Do we have the bacteria or whatever it is that we need to make vinegar?"

"Why do you never tell him no? There's a reason he brings all of his most insane demands to you."

Rowena shrugged. She felt bad for him—he was clearly in over his head. And she was sure he had a good heart, somewhere. "Can we do it or not?"

The treadmill beeped, and Kristen eased into her cooldown. "I'll see what I can do."

They used tomato peels and sugar and water and some bacteria that Kristen assured her was safe for human consumption.

The mayor wasn't happy with the four-week timeframe, but he did beam when Rowena presented him with a jar of tangy red liquid. "Thank goodness, the chef refused to make a backup plan for the shareholder dinner."

Rowena had assumed that the mayonnaise would be for the crew. The shareholder dinner hadn't even crossed her mind. "You're sending it to Earth? Why couldn't they just get supplies down there?"

"Oh don't be silly! We have to give the shareholders an authentic experience!" He floated away, chortling to himself about how pleased his uncle would be.

Her sympathy for him evaporated. Wherever his good heart might be, it would never be on the station. And with him as her boss, she'd never have time for her work.

Something had to be done.

*

Rowena joined Kristen at the treadmill again. "How much vinegar do you think we could make?"

Kristen shrugged. "Lots."

"How much do you think people planetside would pay for space vinegar?"

A slow grin spread over Kristen's face. "Lots."

*

They quietly sold vinegar and bought shares till they had more than the mayor's uncle. They made their case to the board, who finally had to listen to them. Then Rowena went to the mayor's office.

He floated behind his desk, playing a handheld game that he stuffed into a pocked when Rowena entered.

"I'm here to tell you to pack your bags," she said. "You're fired. There's a shuttle leaving in an hour and I want you on it."

"You can't do that!"

Rowena just smiled. "I can, actually. And I have you to thank for the idea. It's the only time you've ever inspired us."

He looked like a kicked puppy, but Rowena didn't care. He wasn't her problem anymore.

Once he was gone, she got back to work. After all, the only thing better than getting to do astrobotany was to do it as her own boss.

Bonus Story 4

This is another one that I wrote for something specific, but I forget what. I like how optimistic it feels.

Progress

Quickly melting snow crunched beneath Leslie's boots as she wandered between the mycology field's carefully placed rotting logs. She spotted a cluster of white fruiting bodies sprouting ahead and quickened her pace.

She brushed snow off the springy caps and harvested them with her hooked knife. Her gathering basket beeped as she dropped them in, confirming that they were edible oyster mushrooms.

She gathered till her basket was full, then headed back to the outpost's main lodge.

Colin greeted her with a quick kiss and a hot cup of hemlock tisane. She gladly traded it for her basket and sat at the kitchen table while he ran the mushrooms through decontamination. "Do you know what today is?" he asked.

"Tuesday?" she guessed.

Colin never had the patience to make her guess twice. "It's mail day."

"Are we expecting anything?" Leslie didn't really pay much attention to supplies that had to be ordered-in. She was only responsible for things that could be farmed or foraged, so those were what she cared about.

"I splurged and put my personal allotment toward some sugar and chocolate. I've almost got the acorn flour brownies right, and Laura's birthday is coming up."

Leslie usually just let her personal allotment roll into the community's Federal funds. Though she was going to need some new hiking boots in the next season or two.

"The protein resynthesizer should finally get here, too," Colin added.

Leslie scowled. "I still can't believe that we voted in favor of that thing."

"It's progress! And a useful tool."

"It lets us eat rotten food. Which is just gross."

"Gross or not, protein is important. And you're a much better forager than Gary is a hunter."

"I still think a second hunter would be more beneficial. Someone else might be able to teach Gary a few tricks."

"And who would you have us trade for this new hunter?"

Leslie sighed. She'd already lost this fight. Not that she'd ever played her last card, because she knew Colin wanted a child, and soon, even if she was more than willing to wait. Or put it off indefinitely. She still wasn't sure if the world was a good place for a baby.

She stood up. "I'm going to go gather some more hemlock needles. Are you going to need help setting the resynthesizer up?"

"It would be appreciated."

"Then I'll head back when I see the mail drone."

*

Leslie stopped for a lunch break in the green quiet of the hemlock grove and idly checked the weather on her tablet.

The forecast was dramatically different than it had been this morning, but that wasn't uncommon. The weather patterns were still shifting. What was surprising was the new estimated low temperature.

She closed the window and loaded it again, but it still displayed an estimated low of negative 18 degrees F. She was appropriately dressed for the current weather—33 degrees and mostly cloudy, but the temperatures were going to be dropping fast.

She sent a quick message on the community-wide channel, grabbed her foraging basket and ran.

*

By the time she got back to the lodge, her breath was misting and her fingers ached from the cold. Laura and Gary were herding the last of the chickens into the one heated barn with the other livestock, and Colin and a few of the others were unloading the mail drone.

"Thanks for the heads up!" Gary called as Leslie jogged up. "Talk about a crazy forecast! I don't know if I've ever seen temperatures that low!"

Leslie had, but she was a good ten years older than Gary, and he'd grown up in one of the domed cities. She reminded herself of that fact when she went inside and saw that all he had to show for his three-day hunting trip was a pair of squirrels.

She thought longingly of venison, of the days when deer had still been so overpopulated that you saw them everywhere. She stored the hemlock needles that she'd gathered in their tub next to the dehydrator, then everything went dark.

She followed the sound of frantic swearing to the dining room, where a small group of people gathered around the new resynthesizer.

"It requires a dedicated higher amp plug. It came with wiring and a new fuse. How did you even get it plugged into a normal outlet?" Colin was just managing to keep his voice even as he examined the wiring.

Lee, another one of the community's younger members, shrugged. "I just grabbed an adaptor."

122

Colin sighed. "I've got to go check and see if the fuse is just blown, or if it's burned out."

Leslie grabbed a flashlight and followed him. "Do we have a replacement if it's burned out?" she asked, careful to keep her voice low.

"Let's see how bad the damage is before we worry," he said.

"I bet it's bad," Leslie said.

Colin opened the fuse box, and they surveyed the damage. "I hate it when you're right," he muttered.

"We're not getting the power back on today, are we?"

Colin shook his head.

"The wood stove in the old barn still works. We have enough wood, and we have plenty of blankets."

"It'll be a tight fit, cramming all of us and the livestock in there."

"More body heat," Leslie said.

"Okay. Let's get everyone moving—it's only going to get colder out there."

*

Everyone piled into the barn and huddled together for warmth. It reminded Leslie of the first few years after the collapse, when cold snaps were a constant threat and all they had was a wood stove and a few cows and chickens. Before allotments and mail drones and reliable wireless access.

The wind howled as the temperature plummeted. Leslie expected the younger people to start complaining any second.

Instead, Gary pulled his guitar out of its battered case. "Who's up for some music?" he asked. No one immediately objected, and he launched into a cheerful camp song. Before Leslie knew it, everyone was clapping and singing along.

They had stew heated on the woodstove and bread toasted on long sticks for dinner, then most people turned in, piling blankets and sleeping bags over piles of hay. Leslie and Colin stayed by the fire—someone had to keep it fed all night.

Gary and Lee sat down next to them. "We can watch the fire for a bit if you two want to sleep," Gary said, his voice low. "We can take shifts," Lee added. "That way, everyone can get some sleep."

"Good idea," Leslie said. "Years ago, when we had our first cold snap, no one managed to get much sleep at all for three days while we waited for it to warm up. Letting someone else tend the fire will be a nice change."

Colin chuckled. "That cold snap was the first time you made me hemlock tisane, and I thought you were plotting to kill me."

123

Gary grinned. "I thought that the first time she made me some, too."

Leslie rolled her eyes. "Hemlock and poison hemlock aren't the same thing."

"We know that now," Colin said.

Gary leaned forward and poked at the fire. "It's not something you learn in the city, though."

"Well, no," Leslie said. "Why would you?" She stood and stretched. "Thanks for taking the first shift with the fire, you two. Wake us up if you need anything."

Gary nodded and looked around the room. He looked older in the firelight. Wiser. Like someone the community could depend on. Maybe that was just wishful thinking. Or maybe it was something she'd been refusing to see.

Leslie slept curled on a pile of hay, nestled in Colin's arms, listening to everyone in the outpost breathing steadily.

No panic, not a word of complaint. She was proud of them.

She made boiled gruel for breakfast. Colin had even thought to grab their tiny supply of coffee, which combated the odor of too-many bodies for at least a moment or two. And all of their combined body heat was actually enough to keep it from being too terribly cold in the barn.

Still, Leslie was glad to get out of the barn when the weather warmed up three days later.

It took another day for the emergency parts they'd requisitioned to arrive, but the mail drone also contained a few packages of spoiled meat to test the resynthesizer out with.

Leslie called the first shower when everything was up and running, and no one complained when she spent fifteen minutes just standing in the hot water.

It was a small luxury, but there'd been a time when she would have called fifteen solid minutes of hot running water an impossible dream.

Maybe, just maybe, a child could do just fine here.

That night, Colin ran the resynthesizer for the first time, and to Leslie's surprise, the results weren't gross at all. A bit on the bland side, but the resynthesized protein would be perfectly pleasant sautéed with some vegetables.

It really was progress, she supposed.

And all things considered, she had to admit that progress was a good thing.

Afterword

Kickstarter was only a fews old when I came up with the idea to try crowdfunding a flash fiction collection. And because of the support of friends and family and even a few fans, I was able to put *One Revolution* together. It was a great experience, but it also took a lot out of me, so I didn't decide I wanted to do it again till 2019.

If I'd known what 2020 had in store, I'm not sure I would have committed myself to writing two stories every month for the year. I lost my job. I got a new one. And then there was the pandemic. But I'm so glad that I did commit myself to writing these stories. This project has been a source of joy for me. And hopefully this book is a way to spread that joy.

I'm so grateful to everyone who backed this project, and I'm especially grateful to everyone who provided a prompt. I love every single one of them, even the challenging ones. I specifically want to thank Chris Aumiller, who increased his pledge at the last minute to make sure the Indiegogo hit its goal, and Todd Sanders, who stepped in to help me with the layout and did an incredible job. I also want to thank everyone who reached out during the course of the year to give feedback on individual stories. It was so amazing and encouraging, and I treasured every message.

Speaking of encouragement, please remember to rate and review this book on places like Amazon and Goodreads if you can.

Hopefully we'll all meet back here for a third trip around the sun.

Thanks again, everyone. I appreciate you.